# There Will Be Wolves

## KARLEEN BRADFORD

**PUFFIN BOOKS**

PUFFIN BOOKS

Published by the Penguin Group

Penguin Putnam Inc., 375 Hudson Street, New York, New York 10014, U.S.A.

Penguin Books Ltd, 27 Wrights Lane, London W8 5TZ, England

Penguin Books Australia Ltd, Ringwood, Victoria, Australia

Penguin Books Canada Ltd, 10 Alcorn Avenue, Toronto, Ontario, Canada M4V 3B2

Penguin Books (N.Z.) Ltd, 182-190 Wairau Road, Auckland 10, New Zealand

Penguin Books Ltd, Registered Offices: Harmondsworth, Middlesex, England

First published in the United States of America by Lodestar Books,
an affiliate of Dutton Children's Books,
a division of Penguin Books USA Inc., 1996
Published by Puffin Books,
a member of Penguin Putnam Books for Young Readers, 1998

1 3 5 7 9 10 8 6 4 2

THE LIBRARY OF CONGRESS HAS CATALOGED THE LODESTAR EDITION AS FOLLOWS:

Bradford, Karleen.

There will be wolves / by Karleen Bradford.—1st American ed.

p. cm.

Summary: Ursula, condemned as a witch because of her knowledge of
healing, escapes being burned to death when she joins her father
and thousands of others who follow Peter the Hermit on
the first Crusade from Cologne to Jerusalem in 1096.

ISBN 0-525-67539-6 (alk. paper)

1. Crusades—First, 1096-1099—Juvenile fiction. [1. Crusades—First,
1096-1099—Fiction.] I. Title.

PZ7.B72285Th 1996 [Fic]—dc20 96-1399 CIP AC

Puffin Books ISBN 0-14-038371-9

Printed in the United States of America

for Jennifer

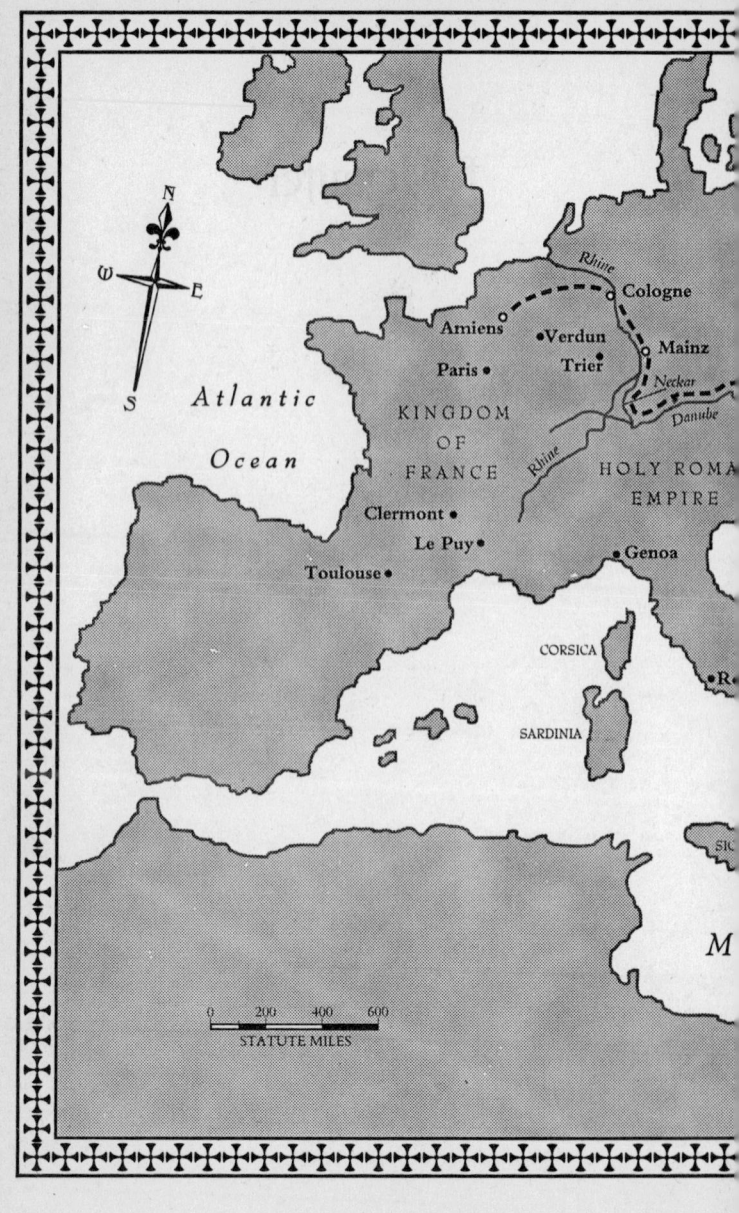

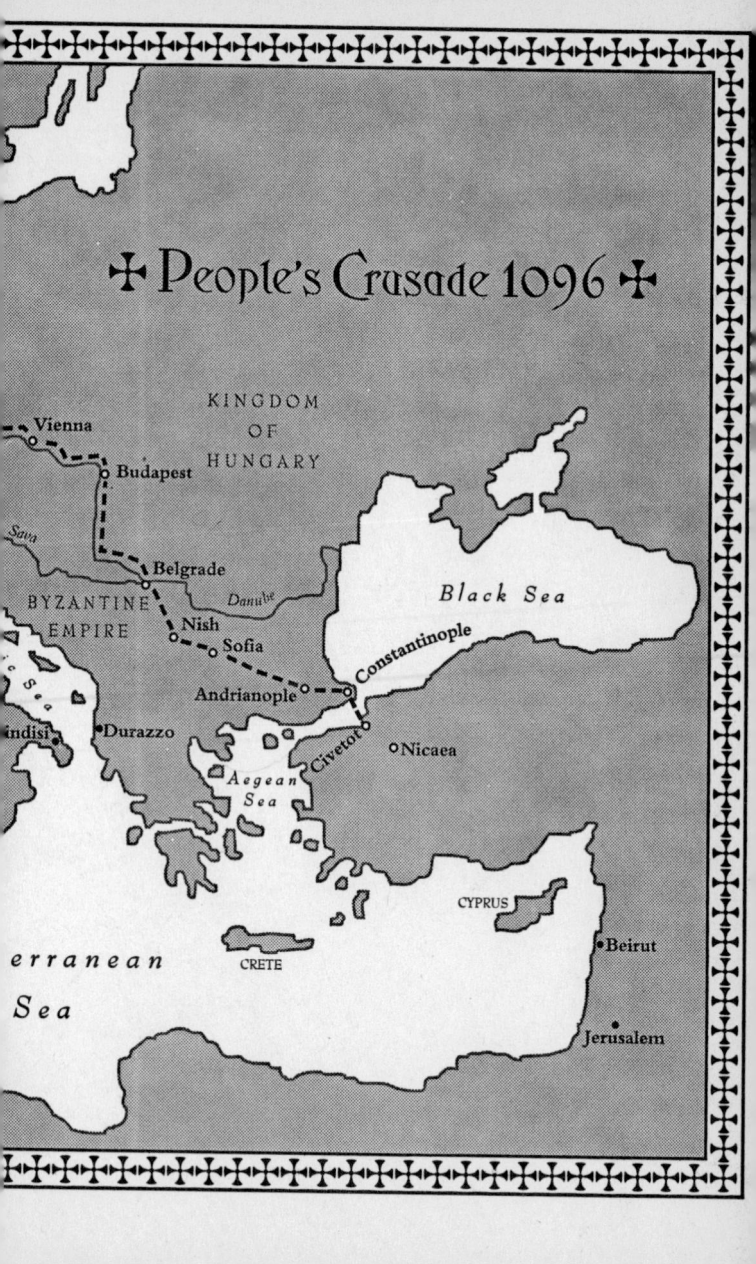

# ✠ People's Crusade 1096 ✠

KINGDOM
OF
HUNGARY

Vienna

Budapest

*Sava*

Belgrade

*Danube*

Black Sea

BYZANTINE
EMPIRE

Nish

Sofia

Constantinople

Andrianople

Civetot

Nicaea

indisi   •Durazzo

*Aegean
Sea*

CYPRUS

*erranean*

CRETE

•Beirut

Sea

Jerusalem

# Prologue

Constantine was the first Christian emperor of the Roman Empire. In the fourth century A.D. he established a new capital for the empire at Byzantium, later known as Constantinople, now known as Istanbul, the capital of Turkey. After the collapse of the Roman Empire, Constantinople survived as the capital of a powerful Christian state, which included the former Near Eastern provinces of the Caesars. This state gradually became known as the Byzantine Empire.

In the meantime, by the eleventh century A.D., a western revival of the Roman Empire had occurred. This empire was called the Holy Roman Empire and comprised all of Germany and northern Italy.

In the middle of the eleventh century, the Byzantine Empire was attacked by the Seljuk Turks, who rapidly overran the eastern provinces, effectively cutting off trade routes and pilgrimage routes to the Holy Land. The emperor, Alexius, sent an appeal to the West to the emperor of the Holy Roman Empire, Henry IV, and to the pope, to help him recapture the Holy Land, most especially the city of Jerusalem. The result of his appeal was Pope Urban II's call for a holy Crusade. There were to be, in fact, several Crusades. The first one of them all, called the People's Crusade, set out for Jerusalem in April 1096 A.D., under the leadership of a monk many believed mad, named Peter.

# Chapter 1

**S**hall I kill him for you?"

"No! I'm going to heal him!" Ursula glared up at the figure standing over her, then moderated her temper as she realized that the words had not been spoken cruelly but with compassion. The dog lying at her feet whined and made a frantic effort to get up. She put out a hand to restrain it.

"But its leg—it seems broken." The boy looked to be only a few years older than Ursula herself. The early spring day was cool, and the wind whipping up from the river cooler still; nevertheless, he was flushed and hot. His rough woolen tunic was disheveled, his fair hair plastered against his forehead; and he seemed to be covered in a kind of fine, white dust.

"It is broken," Ursula answered shortly. "He's been kicked by a horse—belonging to one of Count Emil's men, of course." Her mouth turned down as she glanced along the alley where the man had ridden carelessly off, not bothered in the least by the thought of the injured dog he had left behind. She knew he would have been equally unconcerned even if it had been a child.

"Animals with broken legs don't usually heal. They must be killed." The boy bent toward the dog.

Ursula moved to protect it, but he reached past her and began to quiet the animal. His hands were blunt and work-roughened, the nails broken and torn, but there was gentleness in his fingers. He felt for the wound. "It's the merciful thing to do," he said.

"Not if I can make him well—and I *can*," Ursula countered.

The boy seemed about to argue further, but the look on Ursula's face stopped him. "Shall I help you then?" he asked. "I could carry him home for you."

"I can manage—" Ursula began, then stopped. The dog was much too big for her to carry alone. As she hesitated, a horse-drawn cart clattered toward them through the bustling cacophony of the market stalls, the horse's hooves and iron-rimmed wheels hammering on the cobblestones. It showed no signs of slowing to avoid them. She gave in and nodded.

The boy scooped the dog into his arms and lifted him up. The animal struggled, then relaxed under his soothing.

Ursula stood also and immediately took command. "Follow me," she ordered.

She threaded her way out of one alley and turned into another. This was the street of the tanners and the butchers. The whole city stank, of course, of waste, filth, and rot, but here the smell was overwhelming. Ursula hurried to leave it behind. Around a corner they strode into an even more winding passageway. This was the street of the shoemakers and the saddlers. The upper stories of the houses overhung the roadway so much they nearly touched. Gilded signs swung and creaked in the wind, and apprentices bawled out the wares set on benches before the open doorways. The shouting was tremendous. Then, to add to the noise even further, the bells of all the churches in Cologne began to peal.

Ursula turned to make certain the boy was still following and then continued on, trying to avoid the rivers of sewage that ran down the gutters at her feet. The street of the apothecaries was just around one more corner in this maze. Her father's shop was at the end.

Her father's house was one of the largest: narrow and made of wood, as were the rest, but fully three stories high and with a fine thatched roof. The shutters from the window on the ground floor lay flat upon two trestles to make a counter in front. On this were displayed various bowls and jars of herbs and ointments. Her father stood behind it, pounding a mixture of dried leaves and flowers. He was a thin man, stooped and graying. His face carried lines of loneliness. Ursula's mother had died of the pestilence the year before on the very day Ursula reached her sixteenth year, and all three of her brothers soon after.

He stopped in amazement when he saw Ursula and the boy behind her carrying the dog.

"Child! Whatever is this?"

"A dog, father. Its leg is broken. I must help it."

"And this young man?"

Ursula flushed. In her concern for the animal, she had forgotten all good manners. "He helped me, father. I could not carry the beast alone."

"And his name?"

Ursula flushed even darker. She had never asked.

The boy stepped forward, still cradling the dog. "I am Bruno, master. An apprentice stonemason, working on the new church. I was just on my way home when I saw your daughter—"

"My name is Ursula," she put in quickly and then hurried on, trying to cover her confusion. "The dog— we must see to it. Bring it in here."

She led the way inside the tiny room. Jars and flasks lined the shelves, which covered most of the walls. Bags of all descriptions hung from them. Baskets stood in the corners. The stench of the street was overshadowed here by pungent, even mysterious scents. Against one wall a fire burned in an open hearth. Ursula grabbed a piece of sacking and laid it on the hard-packed dirt floor in front of the fire.

"Put the dog here," she said, "carefully!" as the dog let out a yelp. "Hold him for me now. I must fetch my book and make ready."

Bruno knelt beside the dog while Ursula disappeared up a narrow staircase to a room above. She returned almost immediately, clutching a tattered black book. Her father frowned.

"I do not like you reading in that," he said.

"The old monk gave it to me, father. I've told you so many times—how can it be harmful if it comes from God?"

"It's not right. Young maidens have no business with such things. Brother Bernhard was ill toward the end. He knew not what he was doing."

"Oh, father—" She sighed with frustration. This was an argument that had been repeated often. "He knew exactly what he was doing. He was a healer; he recognized another healer. Besides, you have taught me all that you know of healing herbs and potions— what is the difference?"

"There is a difference. That book is for true healers. Men of age and wisdom. There is more in there than even an apothecary knows. More than an apothecary should know."

Ursula tossed her head angrily, but a pain knotted her chest. A few years back her father would not have spoken so. He had been so brave! So strong! When her mother had objected to him teaching his daughter his trade, instead of his sons, he had defended her boldly. "The boys wish to know nothing of my herbs and the making of healing potions, nor do they have any talent for it. They will find their own work. It is Ursula whom I will train to take my place." And so he had. He had been the best of teachers, interested in everything that was new and eager to learn himself. But in these last few years— Ursula's anger faded, replaced with sadness as she saw how old and defeated he looked now. Suddenly embarrassed as she remembered Bruno's presence, she took the book into the light at the front of the room and began to leaf through the pages.

"Here is what I want," she exclaimed. "How to set and mend a broken bone in a man's arm." Forgetting embarrassment in her enthusiasm, she went on. "If it can be done for a man's arm, why not for a dog's leg?"

"But the dog must walk on it," Bruno objected. He had been watching silently and was looking at the book warily.

"Then we must make it all the stronger." Ursula looked around her, not really paying attention to him or to her father now. She darted over to a wood basket sitting beside the fire; rummaged around among the sticks and bits of kindling until she found two straight, sturdy pieces of wood; and then snatched up a cloth from the corner and tore it into strips. "This should do," she muttered to herself. "But first I must make the poultice. Rosemary and knitbone, am I not right, father?"

Her father nodded, unwilling to speak.

Ursula worked quickly and soon had a sticky, sweet-smelling paste in the old marble mortar. She ground it even more finely with the pestle and then turned back to Bruno. "Now I'll set the bone. Father, will you help?"

With her father and Bruno holding the dog, Ursula

wiped away the blood from the broken skin and felt for the break in its leg. The dog whined and would have moved, but Bruno and her father held it fast. Ursula's fingers moved quickly to straighten the leg; then she reached for the poultice and smeared it over the wound.

"There. Hold the leg for me now," Ursula said to Bruno. "Like this. Hold it steady while I bind it." She placed the two sticks, one on each side of the leg, and bound them securely with the strips of rag. Then she wound more rags over that. Finally she sat back and scrutinized her work.

"Will it mend?" Bruno asked. He looked dubious.

"I don't know," Ursula answered. "But at least he has a chance now. Better that than dead."

Just then a large shape blocked the doorway and a voice rang out. "Master William! Are you not attending to your customers today?"

A woman strode into the room. She wore a cloak the size of a tent over her vast bulk, and its edges swept all before it. Several jars teetered perilously on one of the lower shelves, and a bag fell to the floor. She turned imperiously toward Ursula's father, heedless of the dog, and stepped on its injured leg as she did so. The dog yelped again in pain.

Ursula leaped up. "Mistress Elke! Do be careful!" she cried, reaching out and pushing the woman back.

The woman turned upon Ursula with a glare. "Take your hand away from me, you forward chit! Master William, your daughter forgets herself—as usual!"

"Ursula!" Her father's voice was apprehensive.

"But there's a dog here, a wounded animal. And you trod on him!" Ursula glared back at the woman.

At that moment Mistress Elke caught sight of the book that Ursula had been using. She stepped back quickly; her fingers flew up in the ancient sign against evil. "Do you allow your daughter to read in that?" she demanded, staring at it as if it harbored a nest of snakes. Before Master William could answer, she went on. "That she should be reading at all—a young girl like her—it's against nature. And in that book! It looks like witchcraft to me. You are breeding trouble here, Master William, mark my words!"

"You know nothing of what you speak—" Ursula began hotly, but her father stepped between her and Mistress Elke just as Bruno jumped up and grabbed her elbow.

"The dog," Bruno whispered into her ear. "The bandage has come loose. Perhaps you should see to it."

With a last angry glance at the woman, Ursula allowed herself to be distracted and turned to the animal. Her father hastened to lead Mistress Elke outside.

"Your tisane, mistress," he murmured soothingly. "You'll be wanting your tisane. And how fare you this day? Is all well with you? You mustn't excite yourself, please, mistress. Remember your health. And the health of the innocent babe you carry."

"Innocent babe," Ursula muttered. "A woman like that is more apt to be carrying a demon."

"Hush! Don't speak so," Bruno cautioned, but he was too late; the words had carried out the door.

"What did she say? What did she say?" Mistress Elke screeched. "A demon, she said! She said I'm carrying a demon! She's put a curse on me! Oh, dear God! Holy Jesus!" She staggered and seemed about to faint.

With considerable effort, Master William caught and held her. "No, mistress, no. You misheard. Please, mistress, do not distress yourself. Sit here; I'll prepare your tisane for you this minute. Sit now and calm yourself."

He fetched a stool for her and then rushed back inside to collect his herbs for the tisane.

"Well, now, what have we here?" a voice inquired.

Ursula shuddered. Mistress Ingrid, the busybody who lived in the house next door and whose husband was a rival apothecary, had, as usual, appeared at the first sign of trouble. She bent to Mistress Elke, and a furious avalanche of whispers ensued, with much finger-pointing and many furtive glances at Ursula.

Ursula rose to help her father as she usually did, but she was stopped by another shriek from Mistress Elke.

"No! I won't have her touching anything that is for me! I won't have it, Master William!" She clutched at her bosom with one hand, at Mistress Ingrid's arm with the other.

"Leave us, Ursula," her father ordered, his voice shaking.

"That's my dog."

The voice from the doorway was childish but firm. Ursula looked up to see a boy of about ten or eleven years standing there, staring in. He was small and fine-boned, with a shock of dark, almost black, curly hair falling over his eyes.

"Your dog?" Ursula repeated. She had only just managed to collect herself after Mistress Elke had left. Although she would not have admitted it, Ursula had been frightened. Mistress Ingrid had retired to her own house but was still keeping an obvious watch from her front stoop. Bruno had also left soon after Mistress Elke.

The boy drew himself up proudly. "I am David ibn Shaprut, and that is my dog. He wandered off from me when I was in the marketplace, and, when I inquired, they told me he had been hurt and you had taken him away." His eyes fastened onto the bandaged leg. "Is he hurt badly?" He spoke in the mixture of Hebrew and Germanic dialect, with a few Arabic words thrown in, that the Jews along the Rhine used with the Gentiles. Ursula understood it easily.

Ursula held the dog down firmly. At the first sight of his young master, the animal had begun to whine and try to get up.

"His leg is broken—" she began. Seeing the sudden distress in the boy's face, she added quickly, "But I've set it and put a poultice on it."

"You can't mend a dog's leg if it's broken. Everyone knows that," the boy answered. His eyes became suspiciously bright, but if he was fighting back tears, he didn't let her know.

"Why not? Why not at least try? Come, give him a pat."

David came in and seated himself on the sacking beside the dog. The dog immediately began a frenzy of hand-licking and tail-wagging.

"May I take him home with me?" David asked.

"Not until we know that he's going to be well, I shouldn't think," Ursula answered. "It would be better not to move him."

"And when will we know?" He brushed at his eyes. Ursula pretended not to notice.

"In a few days, perhaps," she said. "In the meantime, can you come by here and keep him company? I'm busy and don't have time to make certain that he doesn't move around too much."

"Yes, I can do that," David replied. The dog had calmed down somewhat, and David continued to stroke his head. "We're here visiting my uncle, my mother and I." He seemed reassured now and began to talk more easily. "My father is a goldsmith—the best goldsmith in Mainz—and so is my mother. She's come to visit my uncle here in Cologne. He's Benjamin ibn Nagdela, a very famous merchant."

Ursula had heard the name often. David's uncle was one of the wealthiest and most successful merchants in Cologne. Or had been, anyway. Cologne had been an important center of trade since Roman times, but ever since the Turks had closed off the trade routes to the East, the merchants were having difficulty. The Jews, in particular, were affected by this, as by Germanic law they were not allowed to own land—not even the land their own houses stood upon—and many of them depended on trade. Ursula had spent countless mornings down at the quayside on the Rhine, watching with fascination as the small but graceful wooden ships sailed in, bringing silks, costly spices, and all manner of things from the East. They were far fewer in number now, however. So few, in fact, that in desperation many of the Jewish merchants had had to resort to moneylending to survive. Many of their Christian fellow townsmen despised them for it. Usury was a sin, according to Christian teachings. Apparently, though, while lending money was sinful, borrowing was not, so many of these same Christians availed themselves of the Jewish money-lenders' services, with the result that they were deeply in debt to them.

For the rest of the afternoon David stayed with his dog, talking to Ursula without pause. Finally, when it was time for the evening meal, he rose to go. The dog made as if to rise and go with him, but David pushed it back down.

"Stay, Samson," he ordered, trying to make his voice as stern as possible.

Ursula suppressed a smile. Samson—one of the most powerful and feared figures in the Old Testament. It was a rather grand name for such a scruffy, nondescript dog.

"I'll be back tomorrow," David promised.

He was. He came with the early-morning hawkers of bread, sweetcakes, and ale—even before the cocks had finished crowing. Ursula had just finished tidying up after breakfast when he appeared at the doorway. For the rest of that morning he stayed, and on into the afternoon, even though he wouldn't share the noon meal with Ursula and her father. Finally Ursula had had enough of his constant chatter, and she seized an excuse to escape.

"I must go to the market and buy fish for our dinner. Will you mind Samson while I'm gone? He mustn't get up any more than necessary." The dog had tried a few experimental steps during the day, keeping his wounded leg well off the ground, but Ursula was anxious that he stay as quiet as possible. She was determined that her efforts to help him would be successful. Then Mistress Elke and all the others like her would see. They'd see that girl or not—young or not—she *was* a healer. That they might not wish to see such a thing flashed through Ursula's mind, but she pushed it away.

Ursula hurried through the twisting streets down to the stalls of the fishmongers in the market by the riverside. She passed the new church that was being built right in the center of all the confusion. Cologne was a city already famous for its churches, and the building of them still went on.

Bruno had said he was an apprentice stonemason working on this church, Ursula suddenly remembered. It was almost finished, but the master stonemason and all the other workers still crowded the courtyard. The choir chamber was yet to be completed. Temporary workshops dotted the area. In one, a blacksmith worked at his forge, making new tools to replace the old iron ones as they wore out. In another, the mortar men made their mixtures of sand, lime, and water to bind the stones together. Pulleys and cranes were still in place, creaking and groaning under the strain of the loads they lifted. Trestles were set up. The shouts of men at work and the noise of sawing filled the open space, and over all—everything and everybody—was the same fine, white dust she had seen on Bruno the day before.

A smaller hut off to one side sheltered the stone-cutters, and it was in front of this that she caught sight of Bruno. He was down on one knee, chipping away at a huge block of stone with a hammer and chisel. Ursula stood watching him, not certain whether she should call out. Suddenly he saw her. He spoke a few quick words to the man next to him and laid down his tools. He then stood up and came toward her, smiling.

"How fares your patient today?" he asked.

"My patient?" Ursula repeated, not understanding.

"The dog. How is its leg?"

"Oh, it's better. Much better. The poor thing even managed to walk a few steps." She smiled back at him. "Its master came for it after you left. He's just a boy. A young Jewish boy called David, from Mainz. Visiting his uncle here."

"Did he take the dog away?"

"No. I told him to leave it with me until we were certain the leg would heal, but he came back today to care for it and hasn't stopped chattering since this morning." Ursula smiled again. "I had to leave for the sake of my ears."

Bruno laughed.

There was a momentary silence. Ursula searched for something to say. "The church," she said finally. "It's very beautiful." She looked up at the pure white stone walls rising above her and glistening in the sunlight. It was built in the form of a cross, with the choir chamber at the eastern end designed in the shape of a cloverleaf. Although not quite finished, the harmony and grace of the building were already evident.

"Would you like to see inside?"

"Oh, yes. Could I?"

In answer, Bruno reached for her hand and drew her into the courtyard. Picking their way through the debris, in and around the busy workers, he led her to the front. Massive bronze doors had been installed, intricately carved with scenes from the New Testament and the figures of the Lord Jesus and his apostles. Ursula reached out a tentative finger and traced their outlines. She had never seen such a marvel.

"That's the master builder's own work," Bruno said proudly. "No other church in Cologne has anything near so fine."

They slipped in and paused for a moment, allowing their eyes to get used to the darkness. No candles were lit yet, of course, so the only light came from the small, deep-set windows. The church was built like a fortress, with walls fully a meter thick. The nave stretched before them, pillars supporting arches that curved up to the domed ceiling above their heads. At the far end the three petals of the cloverleaf opened out into a sweep of such magnitude that Ursula caught her breath. Already the painters had begun their work. The walls and the ceiling challenged the gloom. They were alive with color and shining with gold, brilliantly illustrating stories from the Bible—scenes from Jesus' life and teachings. The floor was patterned with flamboyant mosaics, echoing and emphasizing all the vivid hues around them.

Bruno and Ursula made the sign of the cross toward the place where the altar would soon be and then went farther in. Bruno led her from one painting to another. There was hardly a surface in the whole building that wasn't decorated. What space did remain, Ursula knew, would be covered with hangings and tapestries.

"It's magnificent!" she breathed. "Surely it will be the most splendid church in all of Cologne!"

"It will," Bruno agreed. He dropped her hand and stared around them, his face rapt. "Someday I will build churches, too. Someday I will design them—not just cut stones for them." For a moment he seemed to forget that Ursula was there; he went on talking almost as if to himself. "I have visions," he whispered into the vaulting silence of the empty church. "Visions of churches that reach up to heaven. With high, vast windows that look up to God and let his glory shine in and illuminate everything within. Churches full of light, with pillars and spires that brush the clouds themselves, and with the grace of God celebrated in every stone and every column." He stopped. Then, as if suddenly remembering where he was and with whom, he turned back to her with a laugh.

"I dream," he said apologetically. "Large dreams for one as insignificant as I." He reached for her hand again. "Come. I have finished work for the day. I'll walk with you and you can tell me more about yourself. You called yourself a healer—perhaps you, too, have dreams?"

Ursula looked quickly to see if he was mocking her, but even in the soft dimness of the church she could see only friendship and interest in his eyes.

He kept her company to the fish stalls and waited while she chose the fish for dinner. They then turned back toward her house.

"I would see the dog again," he said, "and perhaps also meet his young master. Would that be all right?"

"Of course," Ursula answered, but a roar from the crowd around them drowned out her voice. They were in the market itself now, and in the very center was a square with a scaffold on it. Here thieves and criminals were punished. On the scaffold was a young man, hardly more than a boy. He was filthy and clad in the barest of rags. His hair hung lank and unkempt over his face and down his back. From where she stood, Ursula could see the wild light of panic in his eyes. Several men stood around him.

As Bruno and Ursula slowed their steps, the men forced the prisoner to kneel and place his hand and arm on a rough wooden block. Ursula could see now that one of the men surrounding the prisoner was holding an axe. As they watched, he raised it high. Another roar came from the crowd.

Ursula felt her arm grabbed roughly by Bruno. "Come," he hissed in her ear. "I want no part of this!"

"But it is only a thief," Ursula answered. "They are only going to cut off a thief's hand." To her surprise, Bruno had turned pale and his mouth was grim.

"His right hand. And what does a man do without his right hand? How will he earn his bread from now on without his right hand?"

The tone of his voice astonished her even more. "But look," she protested. "He's already lacking a finger. He has stolen before. He must have known the punishment. If he valued his hand so much, why did he steal?"

"How do we know? How do we know what has driven the poor wretch to steal? How do we know what he has had to bear?"

"That is of no matter." Ursula dismissed his words with a shrug. "Stealing is a crime. A crime against our fellow men, a crime against God. There's no excuse for it." She knew she was right. "Perhaps this time he will learn his lesson properly. If he repents of his sins and returns to God's laws, those men will be doing him a favor."

The axe paused for a fleeting moment, then flashed down. The young man screamed while the crowd around him cheered. Bruno pulled Ursula away almost viciously.

Ursula gave one backward glance and made a grimace of distaste at the sight of the blood streaming over the block. Then she put the sight out of her mind. She looked curiously at Bruno. He looked as if he would be sick.

"What a strange boy you are," she said.

# Chapter 2

The next day dawned dull and oppressive. There were ominous rumblings of thunder in the air. Ursula looked up at the sliver of sky that she could see between the houses on the narrow street; if it rained she would have to take in all the remedies and herbs she was setting out on the front shutters. David had turned up early again and was sitting with his dog. He was already chattering at full speed—she wondered if he was ever silent. Still, the company was not unwelcome. Her father was feeling unwell and had not yet come down. A stray tabby cat she had been feeding wandered in through the open door and began to wind itself around her feet, mewing softly. The hackles on Samson's back rose, and he growled. David restrained him. The cat, as if realizing that there was no menace from this wounded dog, cast one scornful glance at it and then ignored it.

"You are a brazen little thing." Ursula laughed,

reaching down to scratch it behind the ears. "Two weeks ago you were so wild and unfriendly you wouldn't let me near you, and now look at you, you little beggar. Warm milk in the stomach makes for friendship, it seems, as far as you are concerned." She straightened up, only to see Mistress Elke sailing down the street toward them, her maidservant trailing behind.

No! thought Ursula in a panic. I can't deal with her again. Father will be down in a minute; let him tend to her. She dropped to her knees and crouched below the level of the open window. At the same time the cat, becoming impatient, leaped up onto the shutters. David looked at Ursula in astonishment, but she signaled to him to be silent. It was just possible that Mistress Elke had not seen her—she had been turning her head to chivy her maid when Ursula had caught sight of her. Ursula, feeling slightly foolish, crept on hands and knees through the straw on the floor toward the stairs. Just at that moment, however, Mistress Elke's voice boomed out, loud and strident.

"Fetch your father, my girl. I'll have no dealings with *you*—" The words stopped in midsentence. "Why—? Where did she go? Faith! She was here just a second ago. I turned my head for just a moment, and now she's gone! There's naught here but a cat. The devil himself couldn't have disappeared more quickly!"

Unable to control himself any longer, David began to giggle. Mercifully, Master William came down the stairs just then. He took in the scene, but only shook his head and went quickly over to deal with Mistress Elke. Ursula reached the stairs and darted up them to her room above.

The day passed quietly. It was Good Friday, and all the Christian population of Cologne was preparing for Eastertide. Ursula went to church in the morning, her father in the afternoon. As a devout and humble Christian, he would participate in the dramatic ceremony of creeping to the cross on his knees in the darkened church of Great St. Martin's. Again, David had stayed all day, but this time he had brought some bread and cheese for his noon meal. Being a Jew, he would not share their food. Toward late afternoon, at the time when the workers would be finished and heading for their homes, Ursula found herself glancing more and more often down the street. Without actually admitting it to herself, she was wondering if Bruno would come again. When he did appear, however, she was busy putting her wares away for the night and his voice startled her.

"Hello! Have you heard the news?" he called out as he strode up to the shop. "How goes your dog?" he asked David as he caught sight of him.

"Better, thank you. Much better," David replied with a smile. In fact, the dog had begun to trot around the place almost nimbly. Ursula had renewed the poultices, and the swelling had gone down considerably. There had been no sign of fever at all.

"What news?" Ursula asked.

"There's a holy man camped in the meadow by the Church of the Apostles. Peter the Hermit, they call him. He comes from the Frankish lands, and they say he is telling of wondrous things. Tomorrow, Holy Saturday, he will preach. I intend to go hear him—will you come with me?"

"Yes," Ursula answered. "I would like that. My father also spoke of him and wishes to go. Shall we make our way together, then?"

"By all means. I'll come by early; if we make haste we shall be able to get close enough to hear and see him clearly. They say he has been rousing multitudes since he left his homelands, and a whole host of people follow him. He is preaching a holy pilgrimage—something called a crusade—to liberate Jerusalem from the heathen yoke."

The next morning, Bruno and David arrived together. Leaving David to care for Samson, Ursula, her father, and Bruno set out for the field where the Hermit was to preach. Soon they saw that others were following the same path. People thronged together, the normal excitement of the Easter weekend heightened by this new furor. The talk seemed to be of nothing else but the strange monk and his preachings. Ursula was astonished by the number of people walking along with them but even more astonished when they arrived at the Church of the Apostles. Although the Hermit, also called Little Peter, had not yet arrived, the meadow was already full of his followers, speaking in a bewildering variety of dialects. Most of the dialects were Frankish, but there were others Ursula had never heard before and was at a loss to identify. Many of the people wore red crosses stitched or painted crudely onto their tunics and cloaks.

They had barely arrived when a shout arose from the multitude. Coming up the hill from behind the church straggled a short procession. Leading it was a man seated on a donkey and clad only in filthy rags. He passed directly in front of Ursula. She could see that he was barefoot and unshaven. His beard and long, stringy locks of hair were black, his face dark and sallow. He was as thin as the poor, emaciated beast he rode. As he passed by, people surged forward to touch him, or failing that, to pull hairs out of his donkey's tail to keep as relics. The sparse number of hairs remaining testified to the hundreds of people who had already collected theirs.

"Cured a woman near death with childbed fever, they say!" a woman next to Ursula avowed as she thrust past. "Just one hair!"

Ursula stared at the Hermit with disapproval. In a town situated on a river, and with the number of wells around, there was no shortage of water. Being godly did not necessarily mean being dirty, as far as she was concerned. Beside her, Bruno looked equally unimpressed. Then, as Peter reached the steps of the church, he stopped. He looked around. Seated as he was on the donkey, everyone could see him. The donkey itself drooped disconsolately beneath him as if mourning the loss of its tail hairs. Peter reached both hands out in front of him in a peaceful gesture, but his eyes seemed to flash in the sunlight. There was something both compelling and wild about him. The rabble was silenced almost immediately.

His voice rang out. He spoke in a Frankish dialect, but was echoed instantly by a translator in the Germanic dialect that was most common along this part of the Rhine. The effect was doubly impressive.

"I come with a message from God!" The two voices seemed to fill the meadow. "I come to call you into God's service! Our brethren in the East are crushed and dying under the yoke of the infidels. Our churches are being desecrated. Jerusalem itself—holiest of all cities—is lost to us!" There was an intensity and magnetism about the Hermit as he spoke that was almost hypnotic.

Ursula found herself caught up in it. Gradually, as she listened, she forgot it was the translator's words she heard, forgot her first impressions of distaste. She felt as if Peter's words were being etched directly onto her brain. Around her, the immense crowd was equally spellbound.

The Hermit paused and then began again, even more urgently. "Our fellow Christians cry for our help! Our blessed pope, chosen by God himself, has called upon us to answer their cry. He has called for a Crusade—a holy Crusade—to force a way through to Jerusalem and liberate our brethren. I am answering that call, and you will answer it with me! Many already follow me; many more must join." He paused again. There was a stir in the crowd, but still no one spoke.

"Men, women, children, noblemen, serfs, beggars, even thieves and criminals, join me! Pope Urban has promised absolution to every one of you who participates in this venture. Forgiveness of all your sins! Your lives will be washed clean, your place in Heaven assured! After we have succeeded in God's holy work, you will return pure to a new life. New lands will be yours for those of you who wish to stay. The way to Jerusalem will be open to all of us again. Jerusalem will be *free!*"

At this, as if released from their hypnosis, a roar went up from the people assembled around the monk.

"Jerusalem! Jerusalem!" The cry grew louder and louder.

Ursula was shocked into awareness of what was going on. She looked around her with growing uneasiness as the noise reached a frenzy. Instinctively, she reached for her father's arm. When she turned to look at him, however, he was still staring at Peter as if mesmerized. At that moment Peter raised his hands again, and, although this time it took several moments, at last the people quietened.

"At the end of the month," he commanded. "At the end of this, the month when we mourn Christ's death and celebrate his own glorious Resurrection, we will gather and we will set out on our quest. Leave your homes. Leave your debts and your cares and your tiresome, troubled lives. Join me to march for God and to slay any who would oppose us. The cross, red as the blood of our crucified Savior, will be our symbol. Victory is certain to be ours. *God wills it!*"

The clamor of the crowd rose again, louder than before, and now there was no quelling it. *"God wills it! God wills it!"* Then, the mob began to surge toward the man on the donkey. Only the actions of a gang of strong body servants were able to clear a path for the Hermit as he rode off.

Ursula found herself shoved roughly from behind. She clung even more tightly to her father's arm. She heard him gasp as he, too, was pushed and forced up against the bodies in front of them. Her face was pressed into a sweating, roughly shirted back, and for a moment she panicked, almost suffocating. The jostling of the people around her caused her to lose her footing. She regained it but realized with sudden horror that her father had fallen. She lost her grip on his arm, and before she could help him, the crowd swept her out of reach.

"Father!" she screamed. A hand grabbed at her, and she yanked herself away in terror.

"Ursula! It's me!"

The hand caught hold of her again and she recognized Bruno. "Father!" she cried. "He's fallen!"

Bruno squeezed past her. By dint of sheer strength, he elbowed his way through to the older man and shielded him with his body as he helped him rise. Ursula managed to get to him as well. Then the three of them fought their way to the edge of the heaving mass.

"Come," Bruno said, not allowing them time to rest. "We must get out of here. This is an insanity."

They made their way out of the meadow, but even then could not get completely away from shouting, wrought-up people. The streets of the city itself were crammed, and all normal business had come to a halt.

"I've never seen people like this." Ursula panted as she helped her father along behind Bruno. "I can't understand it."

They were near the Jewish section of the city. Ursula recognized a respected Jewish scholar and his wife coming toward them. At the same time, a knot of men pushed past her from behind. Ursula could smell the stale odor of beer and wine, mixed with sweat and filth. The men were dressed in coarse woolen cloaks with flaming red crosses roughly painted on the shoulders. As they came abreast of the Jewish couple, the leader reached out and pushed the old woman aside. His companions, following his lead, forced the man to stumble into the gutter.

"Out of the way, Jews!" the leader cried. "Killers of Christ! Make way for those who would defend him!"

The man reached out instinctively to protect his wife, but the leader knocked him flat with one blow. Ursula heard her father exclaim in horror. She watched as the men strode off, laughing and shouting triumphantly, and then she and Bruno ran forward to assist the couple.

The elderly man picked himself up and dusted himself off with dignity. He reached for the hand of his wife, who was sobbing helplessly, and comforted her.

"I am not hurt, my love, do not distress yourself. But Bishop Hermann will hear of this. The archbishop of Cologne is a good friend to the Jews in this city, and he will not tolerate such indignities." He turned to Ursula and Bruno. "Thank you, my children, for your concern, but we are perfectly all right."

With a courteous bow to Master William, they continued on their way. Ursula stood looking after them. She was shaking with anger as she reached for her father's arm again, but mixed in with it was fear. What was happening here? She turned to her father. He was staring after the man and his wife, obviously dazed and still confused about what had happened.

"I need a draft of wine to wash the taste of this out of my mouth."

Bruno's voice startled her. She looked at him quickly. On his face was the same expression he had worn when he had seen the thief about to lose his hand. Then he turned to them, and his face changed as he saw Master William's distress.

"Your father needs a place to sit and rest himself. My hut is close by. Will you come?"

Ursula felt a great need to sit down herself. She nodded wordlessly.

The old Roman wall still protected Cologne, and Bruno's hut, made of wattle and thatch, was built up against it on the southern side of the city, near one of the gates. There was no window, and the only light came from the door, which he left open. Ursula squinted into the gloom as she entered. As her eyes grew accustomed to the dark, she saw a straw pallet in one corner of the room. A coffer sitting against the far wall and a small trestle table were the only other pieces of furniture. The floor was hard-packed earth with a few fresh rushes strewn over it. The remains of a fire nestled up to the ancient stones of the wall. An opening cut into the roof above let in practically no light but hopefully would let out the smoke when the fire was lit.

Bruno led Master William over to the coffer. Exhausted, the older man sank down onto it. Ursula sat beside him.

"Will you have wine, master?" Bruno offered. He picked up a flask and poured from it into a horn. Ursula's father accepted it gratefully.

"Are you hungry?" A bit of stale cheese and the remains of a loaf of black bread sat on the trestle. Bruno brushed a swarm of flies off them. "Would you like something to eat?"

Master William shook his head. "Thank you, no. I will just rest a moment—that's all I need."

Bruno looked to Ursula.

"No!" Ursula blurted out. "Thank you," she added hastily. She would have to be starving indeed before she ate leftover food such as that!

Bruno flushed. "My hut is rather poor," he said stiffly, "but at least it is the hut of a free man."

Ursula was startled. It hadn't occurred to her that he might be otherwise.

"My parents are country people," he explained, "serfs belonging to Count Emil. Half their yearly harvest, poor as it is, must go to him. There was not enough to feed all the hungry mouths at home, so I left and came to the city. By God's grace it was found that I had a talent with stonework. Now, after having lived in the city for a year, I am granted my freedom and so am no longer Count Emil's man, but my own."

Ursula nodded, for a moment at a loss as to what to say, but then she returned to the subject that was uppermost in her mind. The figure of Peter the Hermit was still before her, and his words still echoed. "What thought you of the preacher?" she asked.

"A strange man," Bruno answered. "And strangely compelling. Dangerously compelling."

"Why say you that?" Master William broke in.

"I liked not what he had to say," Bruno answered. "He stirs people up for this Crusade, saying it is a holy venture, and yet he speaks of killing. True Christians cannot kill. It is a sin."

"But it is in God's name," Master William protested. "To further God's will. To liberate our brethren in the East!"

" 'Thou shalt not kill.' Is that not one of the Commandments?" Bruno answered. "Our Lord Jesus never took arms against any man, and yet he wrought more change in our world than anyone else before him."

"But the pope himself has called for this. Are

you condemning the pope?" Master William staggered to his feet, wine spilling from the horn in his hand. "This Peter is a holy man. He may be a saint! Are you saying he is not preaching God's word?" The hand holding the horn of wine began to shake, so Bruno had to grab for it. Master William's face flushed and his watery blue eyes shone suddenly as if with tears.

"Father! Calm yourself!" Ursula sprang up and reached to steady him.

"I am saying I cannot believe that a true Christian should ever kill," Bruno answered, his face anxious but his voice stubborn. "It goes against all that we are taught."

"This Crusade is a holy thing. A holy thing—" Master William insisted, but his voice was thready and weak. His whole body began to shake.

"You are upsetting him," Ursula snapped. "Can you not see what you are doing?"

"And do you agree with what the monk preached?" Bruno challenged her. "He is preaching violence, not brotherly love. Violence breeds violence, and it is hard to contain once lit."

"I know not what I agree with. I know only that my father is in distress. Thank you for your wine. We will go home now."

But as she led her father through the alleys to their shop, she could not rid herself of the memory of the old Jewish couple being pushed into the gutter.

"Violence breeds violence." Bruno's words echoed in her mind. "And it is hard to contain once lit."

"Would that I could go on such a Crusade," Master William said wistfully as they entered their home. "Would it not be wonderful, Ursula, to see Jerusalem and to be one of the number that set it free for all Christians again?"

Ursula looked at David, sitting silently by the fire patting Samson, and did not reply.

The next day, Easter Sunday, was a day usually spent in prayer and celebration. Ursula and her father joined with their neighbors in the procession that wound through the city to the Bishop's Church, but it worried her that the rough crowds of strangers bearing their red crosses still thronged the streets, drinking and carousing.

By Monday morning things at first seemed to be back to normal. Then, just as Ursula was beginning to prepare the noon meal, Bruno burst through the door. David, who was sitting by the fire, leaped to his feet, startled. Samson let out a low growl before he realized who it was.

"There are riots!" Bruno announced. "The Crusaders have been working themselves up all weekend, and now they are searching out all the Jews they can find and crying that the killers of Christ must be punished before the Crusade can begin. People are hiding them, and the archbishop has given sanctuary to as many as he could in the Bishop's Church, but the mobs are out of control."

"I must get back to my uncle's house!" David cried. He started for the door.

"It is too late. The streets are full—you would be struck down at once," Bruno answered.

"Stay here, David," Ursula said, stopping him. "Your mother and your uncle will be with the archbishop, I'm sure. You'll be safe here."

"I'm not even certain of that," Bruno answered. "This is a rabble, and it has gone wild. They are forcing their way into private houses to seek out any hidden Jews and dragging them into the streets."

"I *must* go!" David cried again.

"You will never make it. The crowd was following behind me as I came." As if to prove Bruno's words, distant shouting could be heard coming rapidly closer.

"We must hide him," Ursula said desperately. "Quickly, up the stairs into the loft!"

"No—there is a better place." Master William spoke for the first time. The others looked at him, surprised. "David, quickly now, follow me down into the cellar."

Ursula stared at her father, startled by the unaccustomed note of sharp authority in his voice. David turned to obey him.

"The cellar! Father, there is no hiding place there!" Her father didn't answer, but hustled David toward the trapdoor set into the floor in the far corner of the room.

Before Ursula could recover from her astonishment, they disappeared down it together, and her father pulled the wooden planking closed behind them. Almost at the same time a wave of rioting, shouting men broke into their narrow alley. Ursula and Bruno ran to the doorway and watched, aghast, as the mob surged toward them. Five broke off from the rest and pushed past the others into the house. Bruno tried to stop them but was knocked to the floor. Samson growled, in earnest this time, and sank his teeth into the leg nearest to him. A kick sent him sprawling, yipping with fresh pain. Ursula felt herself grabbed and thrust against the wall.

"It is said that you harbor a Jew here—where is he?" the leader demanded. His heavy, bearded face was only inches away from her own, and the stench of rotting teeth sickened her. She wondered briefly how they had found out about David, then knew. Mistress Ingrid, no doubt, had been quick to provide the information.

Bruno made an effort to rise and was knocked down again. His head hit the stones of the fireplace, and he lay suddenly still.

"A Jew boy! He comes every day. Where is he?"

"He—he came not today," Ursula managed to get out.

"You're lying! You're hiding him!" The man shook Ursula against the wall so violently she felt her head swim.

"No," she gasped. "He came not today," she repeated.

"We'll soon see about that!" With a wave of his hand, he sent two men toward the stairs. He held Ursula, and she watched as they disappeared from sight. There were curses and sounds of stools and coffers being thrown around. Then they came back down.

"No one there."

"I know he's here somewhere." The leader loosed Ursula and looked around thoughtfully. "There must be a cellar. There!" He pointed triumphantly to the trapdoor and sprang toward it.

Ursula let out an involuntary cry.

"Aha! No Jew, eh?" He threw back the door and disappeared down the steps.

The cellar was a vast room where Ursula and her father stored vegetables and their supplies of herbs and ointments. It was old, far older than the house itself, full of arched nooks and crannies. The walls were carved with grotesque heads of mythical beasts and wild animals. Dark and dank, it was even frightening, but there were no hiding places there; Ursula knew that. Not even for a small boy. Certainly not for a small boy and an old man.

# Chapter 3

Ursula stared at the open trapdoor and waited for the shouts of discovery. Incredibly, there were none. Instead, the men trooped back up, looking confused and angry.

"I could have sworn—" the leader began. Then he scowled at Ursula. "It seems you speak the truth. I would have lain down my life that there was someone hidden there." He pushed past her and strode out the door, his gang of ruffians close behind him.

Ursula made a move toward the open door, but just then Bruno groaned. She went over to him quickly and knelt to help him. He sat up groggily, holding his head with both hands. Beside him, Samson whimpered and scrabbled closer.

"Are you all right?" Ursula asked anxiously.

"I'm not sure," he answered. "My head hurts." He tried to stand but then sat back down. "My head certainly *does* hurt," he repeated. Then he seemed to come to his senses. "What happened?" he asked. "Where are those men? Did they find David?"

"They've gone," Ursula answered. "Father took David and hid in the cellar. I don't know why they didn't find them—there is no hiding place down there—but somehow they didn't."

"Maybe you underestimate your father, my dear."

Ursula looked up in surprise to see Master William emerging from the trapdoor, David close behind. Her father had a triumphant smile on his face.

"Father! Where . . . ?"

"Don't you remember the stories about this house, daughter?" her father answered. He turned to Bruno. "When our Emperor Henry was but a small boy, the archbishop of Cologne—Bishop Anno it was then—had him brought here to Cologne and hid him away. The archbishop's desire was to control the emperor and thereby gain power over the Holy Roman Empire itself, of course, and for a while he was successful. No one could discover where he had hidden the boy king, but rumor has it that it was in this very house. I for one am inclined to believe it, although Ursula scorns the idea. What think you now, daughter?" Master William looked positively gleeful.

"Where were you?" Ursula demanded. "I *know* there's no hiding place down there."

"But obviously there is. David knows now, don't you lad?" The old man laughed and, to Ursula's fury, would say no more.

David sank down beside Samson. "When do you think I can return to my uncle's house?" he asked, with a worried look at Bruno.

"Stay here for now," Bruno answered. He tried to rise again and this time managed it, although with a grimace of pain. "I'll go find out what is happening, but in the meantime you must stay out of sight. I don't imagine those men will be back, but don't let anyone else see you. We know not who is a friend and who is an enemy in this case."

"He's right, David. If Mistress Elke or that busybody next door happened by and saw you, the tale would be all over town in minutes that you are still here. Run upstairs and keep out of sight. We'll let you know when it is safe for you to go out."

Reluctantly, David headed for the stairs. Bruno made as if to leave, but Ursula stopped him.

"Before you go, let me tend to that bump on your head. You gave it a fair crack, I think."

Bruno started to protest, but no one argued with Ursula when she had her mind made up. Back in command of herself and the situation, she pushed him down onto a straw pallet in the corner; poured out a mug of boiling water from the pot hanging over the fire; and, after consulting her healing book, threw in a handful of herbs.

"Lavender for the pain and rue for dizziness," she explained as it brewed. When she judged it to be ready, she handed the mugful of concoction to Bruno. He sipped and made a face. "Drink it," Ursula commanded, "while I make a poultice for the bump. Catmint helps bruises."

By the time Bruno forced the drink down, Ursula had the poultice ready. A large, ugly bump was coming up on his forehead, just above the right eye. Ursula felt it gently and then began to smooth and rub the catmint paste over it. Bruno winced but remained silent.

Suddenly the stray cat appeared. It sidled over to Ursula and began to wind itself around her ankles more and more excitedly. Ursula laughed. "You smell the catmint, do you, you rascal? Well, have some then." She put a small amount of the paste on the tip of one finger and rubbed it on the cat's paw. Immediately the cat went into a frenzy of rolling, licking, and pouncing at imaginary mice. Totally ignoring Samson, who was whining indignantly in the corner while being held back with some difficulty by Master William, the little cat was soon in a delirium of delight.

"I'll go now," Bruno said finally when Ursula had bound his head to her satisfaction. "Keep David out of sight, and I'll return as soon as possible."

No sooner had he left than Ursula heard excited voices approaching. A group of girls her own age paused by the trestle where the herbs were displayed. Ursula's book lay open among the bowls.

"What think you of all the commotion, Ursula?" one of them, a bright-eyed, pert girl, asked. "It seems to have calmed down now, and we're off to the marketplace to gather news—will you come?"

Ursula looked at them in dismay. If David should appear—

"No, Britta," she answered quickly. "I have no time for that. I have work to do." Her thoughts were with David, and the words were abrupt, even rude.

The girl's face darkened. "Truth, I forgot. You are not like the rest of us useless things, are you? You are an *important* person." Her voice dripped sarcasm; then her eyes fell on the book. "A *clever* person," she went on. "A person who can *read*. Of course you don't have time for us and our foolish talk." She tossed her head and turned to the others. "Come away, then. Mistress Ursula has work to do."

Ursula bit her lip, then shrugged. She knew Britta and the other girls her age resented her and found her proud, but she really had nothing in common with them. Gossip and the pursuit of a husband were all they seemed to care about.

It was several hours before Bruno came back, and when he did, his face was pale.

"What is it?" Ursula asked with a sudden terrible sense of misgiving. "What has happened?"

"Is David still here?"

"Yes. What's wrong?"

"Something terrible." Bruno shook his head slowly from side to side. "Something terrible," he repeated. With an effort he straightened up. "I must go to David. I must tell him."

But David, who had been watching for him, bounded down the stairs. "Bruno! Have you seen my mother and uncle? Is it safe for me to go to them now?"

Bruno looked at him. He tried to speak, then stopped. He made another effort. "Your mother—" he began. "Your uncle—" He stopped again and closed his eyes as if in even greater pain than before.

"What? What is it?"

Bruno opened his eyes again and drew a deep breath to brace himself. "They're both dead," he said. "All the members of your uncle's household. It seems they didn't make it to the Bishop's Church in time, and they were overrun by the mob."

Master William let out a cry and reached to hold David. David didn't seem to notice. He stared at Bruno unbelievingly. "Dead?" he echoed. "My uncle? My *mother?*"

"Yes."

His face went white. For a moment he stood immobile; then, without another word, he tore himself loose from Master William and disappeared up the stairs. Ursula made as if to go after him.

"It might be best to leave him alone for a while," Bruno said.

"But he will need someone."

"Go to him in a few minutes, but first, listen to me. There's more to tell. Very few of the Jews in Cologne were killed. Most of the citizens did as you and your father did and hid them until the frenzy was over. But David's family—it would seem that the Crusaders had help there."

"What do you mean?" Ursula asked.

"They say that Count Emil himself had a hand in the massacre of David's family."

"I can't believe that!" Master William exclaimed.

"But why—?" Ursula began.

"The count owed a vast sum of money to David's uncle. It might have been a good way to settle the debt."

"That's impossible!" Master William put in. "The count may be a harsh man, but he would not stoop to such a thing."

Ursula's mouth twisted. "I'm not so certain of that as are you, father," she said.

Bruno continued. "The talk is that Count Emil knows there was a boy visiting as well, and he knows that the boy escaped and is hidden somewhere in the city. His own men are looking for David now. David is in more danger than ever."

"Then we'll hide him again!" Ursula said fiercely. "They'll not take David from here—I swear to that!"

"This cannot be true." Master William was shaking his head in disbelief. "You must be wrong, my son. It must just be idle talk and rumors."

"I wish it were, master, but I'm afraid it sounds true to me." Bruno turned back to Ursula. "It might not be so easy to hide David again," he said. Everyone knows that he comes here to see his dog—they'll be back, and they'll search with much greater determination next time."

"They can search all they want. They'll not get David from here." Ursula swung around and ran up the stairs to the boy.

Toward nightfall the streets seemed to quiet down a little. Ursula and Bruno conferred and came to the decision that nothing more was likely to happen until the next morning at least. Bruno left, promising to return as early as possible with whatever the latest news might be. Ursula fixed up a small pallet in the corner of her room for David. She was prepared to defend him with her life, if need be, but for most of the night all she could do was listen to him sobbing. Nothing she could say would comfort him. Finally he seemed to sleep and, exhausted, she did as well.

When Ursula awoke, however, and looked over toward the corner, David was gone. In a panic, she threw back her cover and raced downstairs. Samson was snoozing beside the fire as usual, her father already preparing the morning's work.

"David!" she cried. "He's gone!"

"It's all right," her father answered. "He left during the night."

"Left? Where to?"

"He felt he must go back to his father in Mainz. He had to let his father know what has happened."

"To Mainz? He's going all the way to Mainz by himself? But there are Crusaders roaming all over the countryside—he'll be in terrible danger!"

"I could do nothing to stop him." Master William busied himself with his herbs, his back to Ursula. "His mind was made up. Anyway, by himself he will probably have a good chance. Who pays any attention to one lone boy on the roads? I'm certain he will be all right." He sounded as if he was trying to convince himself as much as Ursula.

"But surely you could have done *something*, father. How *could* you let him go off alone?"

"It was his decision, Ursula. It was not my place to stop him." Master William's voice rose. "Besides, if what Bruno says is true—although I still cannot bring myself to believe it—he would be in worse danger here." He caught himself and then went on with an obvious effort to make his tone calm. "He asked me to bid you good-bye and thank you for your care and help. He couldn't take Samson with him because the dog is not yet well enough to make such a trip, but he asked me to beg you to care for him until he can return for him." In spite of his efforts, his voice trembled. He reached out to straighten some of the herbs on the shutter but only succeeded in knocking a bag onto the floor. He knelt quickly to retrieve it and then looked up at Ursula. His face suddenly seemed to collapse. His eyes stared at her but as if not really seeing her.

"The Crusade," he whispered. "The Crusade is to be a glorious endeavor. How can it be born out of such things? Out of such evil?"

The house was searched repeatedly during the next week, but finally the men who were seeking David were convinced that he had, indeed, fled. Ursula worried and Samson pined, but there was no news of the boy and no real hope that there would be. There was no telling how long it would take him to reach Mainz, if he ever did, or how long it would take him to get word back to them of his safety.

Talk in the town, meanwhile, was of little else than the Crusade. Pope Urban had declared that it would officially start in late August, and most of the nobles and lords from all around the countryside were beginning to make their preparations for leaving at that time. Peter the Hermit, however, had other ideas. He was on fire with enthusiasm to start right away, and a goodly proportion of the people of Cologne were eager to support him. His own following was so large and so unruly—even though there had been no further killing of Jews—that there were mutterings among the less enthusiastic that it would be for the city's own good to have them leave as soon as possible. The archbishop of Cologne, for whatever reasons, supported Peter in his decision. The enthusiasm quickly attained fever pitch. When Count Emil and several of the neighboring lords declared their intention of leaving with Peter as soon as possible, there was no containing the excitement. The town now swarmed with Crusaders; the red cross was seen on nearly every shoulder and breast.

Bruno continued to visit regularly, but he and Master William still disagreed about the Crusade itself.

"I am concerned about my father," Ursula said one day. He had gone as usual to hear Peter speak; he hadn't missed one of the monk's gatherings. "He thinks of nothing else but this Crusade and leaves more and more of his work to me. I believe he has even forgotten the murder of the Jews. It is not like him."

"I agree," Bruno began, but was interrupted by a commotion in the street. He and Ursula looked out the door to see a group of angry women charging toward the house. Ursula was puzzled but relieved to see that Mistress Elke was not among them. Of late, as the time for the birth of her child had drawn near, the woman had taken an even more violent aversion toward Ursula. Whenever she felt ill she blamed Ursula for handling her tisanes and infusions, although the girl was scrupulously careful to avoid them. The last time Mistress Elke had visited their apothecary, she had tripped over Ursula's stray cat and fallen heavily. No amount of soothing or reasoning on the part of Master William had been able to convince her that Ursula had not had a hand in it.

Ursula's relief was short-lived.

"Witch!" the women shrieked as they advanced in a solid, hate-filled body toward her. "Witch!"

Ursula stood, astonished, as they drew up in front of her and brandished their fists.

Bruno instinctively took a step forward as if to shield her. "What is the meaning of this?" he demanded.

"Mistress Elke's babe was born dead and monstrously deformed—like a demon!" one of the women screamed.

"It's all this girl's doing—Mistress Elke says so herself!" yelled another.

"That's not possible!" Ursula flashed out the denial, but her heart sank.

"You put a curse on her; admit it!" shrieked a woman. Ursula recognized Mistress Adelheid, the widow of a shoemaker. She was a vicious-tongued virago who, it was widely believed, had scolded and tormented her poor husband even on his deathbed. She seemed to be the leader of the group.

Mistress Ingrid from next door, ever alert, rushed out to see what was going on and joined the group immediately.

"That's right," she chimed in. "She said Mistress Elke was carrying a demon."

The women crossed themselves hastily.

"And she turned herself into a cat one day—I saw it myself! Only a witch could do that!" Mistress Elke's serving girl, usually meek and craven, was emboldened by this furious group, and shouting just as loudly as the others, her face just as contorted.

"That's not true!" Ursula cried out. She began to shake. "I did nothing!"

At that moment Master William appeared. He stared at the group of women in confusion. "What—? What is going on?"

"Your daughter is a witch, Master William, and we'll prove it!"

For a moment it seemed as if the women would surge forward and seize Ursula right then and there, but her father, still bewildered, moved between them.

"Witch!" The cry was raised once more.

"Witch! Witch!" The others took it up, but there was no one willing to push past Master William.

"You've not heard the last of this, my girl," Mistress Adelheid screeched finally. "Nor have you, Master

William. We're decent folk here, and we'll not have the likes of this going on. The archbishop himself will hear of this. He will decide what's to be done."

Master William stared at the women unbelievingly. Most of them had known and been treated by him for years; they had been friends and neighbors to his family for most of their lives. "My ladies," he began feebly, "there must be some mistake—"

"There's been no mistake, and the archbishop will not tolerate the devil's work in his own city!" a voice shrieked at him in return.

"We'll be back," Mistress Adelheid promised. "We'll be back and then we'll see what's to be done." She whirled and strode away, with the crowd of muttering women following close behind.

Ursula looked past her father to Bruno. "I cannot believe this," she whispered, but a sick, twisting pain knotted her stomach, and she recognized it as fear.

That night Ursula was awakened by a strange smell and the sound of Samson barking frantically at the bottom of the stairs. It took her a moment to collect herself, and then she realized that the room was rapidly filling with smoke. She sprang off her pallet and screamed to her father, who slept on the floor above. When he didn't answer, she raced for the ladder that connected the second floor to the third and was up it in an instant, shaking him awake.

"What? What is it, child?" The old man was vague with sleep and almost incoherent. He had been so upset by the women that Ursula had insisted he take a potion to help him rest. Now he could not seem to waken.

She shook him harder. The smoke was getting thicker, reaching up even to this floor, and the acrid taste of it in the back of her throat was making her cough.

"Fire, father! The house is on fire! Oh, father, wake up! We must run!"

Samson was howling now. Master William sat up, still dazed, and Ursula dragged him to his feet. She pushed him over to the hole where the ladder was and thrust him toward it. He barely managed the rungs. Then she put her arm around his shoulders and helped him down the stairs. Samson was in a frenzy.

The bottom floor was ablaze; flames licked at the shelves with their store of dried herbs. Ursula seized her father tightly and fought her way through the smoke to the door, but she had to let go of him in order to open it, and he sank onto the floor. She pulled the door open, reached down, and half dragged, half carried him out. Samson charged out behind them.

Then Ursula remembered her book—her healing book. She dropped her father's arm and raced back into the house, ignoring the shouts of the people who were already collecting at the scene. The smoke was almost overpowering, but she ran for the stairs and pulled herself up them. The book was in a corner under her bed. Coughing, with tears streaming down her face, she reached for it. The whole wall beside her was in flames and the heat scorched her hand. She grasped the book and then almost fell back down the narrow stairway. As she staggered out the door, the floor of the second level crashed down behind her.

The entire neighborhood was awake by now, and shouts were being raised all along the street. Men raced up carrying buckets of water from the nearby well and began to throw it on the fire, but the smoke was too dense, and the heat of the flames soon drove them back.

"Watch out! The roof's going!" Even as the shout was raised, the whole top of the house caved in, sending up a towering blaze that leaped for the sky. Now all the efforts of the dozens of people in the street were directed to wetting down the adjoining houses on either side in order to prevent the fire from spreading. Ursula could do nothing but stand with her arms around her father and watch as everything they owned in the world went up in flames.

By the time the first light of day began to streak through the sky, it was all over. Their house was an empty, smoldering shell. Ursula stared at the wreckage. The houses on either side had been burned as well, but not extensively; by and large, they had been saved. People were standing around, staring, or sitting slumped in the street, silent and exhausted. Suddenly a shout startled them all.

"There she is! There's the witch! Look—God has already laid his hand upon her!"

The women were back, but this time, they were led by the monks from the church of Great St. Martin's. One of the monks, surveying the burned-out ruin, crossed himself and began to pray.

"God sent the fire!" shrieked Mistress Adelheid. "The fire that purifies! God sent it!"

"Yes!" cried another. "He's burned the witch's house—and now the witch must burn!"

# Chapter 4

Ursula's arms dropped away from her father and, instinctively, she tried to hide the book. It was too late. The ever-observant Mistress Ingrid had already seen it.

"Look! She clutches the book. The devil's book!" she cried. "Mistress Elke told me about that as well. It's from that book she casts her spells!"

Ursula shrank back, but one of the monks moved toward her quickly.

"Give that to me," he said. In contrast to the turmoil and commotion all around them, his voice was quiet, but it was a voice to be obeyed. Nevertheless; Ursula was not about to give in so easily.

"It's mine," she countered. She faced the monk defiantly, using every effort of will she could summon up to keep her voice steady. Her knees were weak, and the sickening pain was back in her stomach, but her relentless grip on the book kept her shaking hands from betraying her. "It was given to me by a brother from your own order. He was my friend. He wanted me to have it."

The monk stopped short, shocked. "Who? Who from among our community would give a book to you?"

"Brother Bernhard. Just before he died. He was a healer and he knew that I was one, too. He wanted me to have it."

"Child, you are condemning yourself with every word you speak!" The monk turned pale. "If that is indeed Brother Bernhard's book of healing, then you have committed an unpardonable sin. The book disappeared just before his death. It belongs to the church, to God. You have stolen from God!"

"I did not steal it! I am no thief!" Anger momentarily overcame Ursula's fear. "He gave it to me. I would go and talk with him by the river below the church. He knew that I was a healer. He taught me many things."

"Enough! You will give that book to me immediately." The monk stepped forward and held out his hand.

Master William suddenly gasped, clutched his chest, and fell to the ground.

"Father!" Ursula reached for him and dropped the book.

The monk swooped down and picked it up in one quick, hawklike movement. He opened it carefully and looked at it; he then looked back at Ursula, crouching beside her father. "You will come with us," he said.

"But my father—"

"The good people here will tend to him. He has no need of you. You will only do him more harm than good." He turned his back on her and signaled to two other monks. "Escort her."

"No!" Ursula cried.

"Escort her!" the monk ordered again.

The monks flanked Ursula on either side. They did not touch her, but it was clear that they could make her go if she chose to protest. With one last, despairing look at her father, Ursula stood.

"Follow me," the monk commanded.

Ursula forced her feet to move. Her whole body was shaking now so badly there was no longer any hiding it. She began to walk. Just at that moment she saw Bruno turn the corner into their street. Samson trotted down to meet him, tail wagging.

Bruno stopped. Then, seeing what was happening, he rushed forward but was prevented from reaching Ursula by the crowd. Pandemonium broke loose. The women, who had fallen silent when Master William collapsed, burst into noise again as they surrounded him. Above the din one voice rang out.

"Now we'll see justice done!" shrieked Mistress Adelheid. "Now we'll see the witch pay for her sins!"

When Ursula awoke the next morning, she lay for a moment, confused and disoriented. Cocks were crowing outside as usual, but everything else was wrong. No light filtered in through the oiled sheepskin-covered window at the foot of her straw pallet as it ordinarily did. The blanket covering her was thin and scratchy and smelled sour. She almost panicked—then she remembered. The monks had brought her to the nuns at St. Maria Lyskirchen. She had been shut into a narrow, windowless cell and left there for the rest of the day. Except for one nun who had brought her some bread and a bowl of thin gruel that she hadn't been able to eat, and another who had come to empty the pail that stood in the corner, she had seen no one. They had let her have a wick floating in tallow for a light. As long as that lasted, she had paced the room restlessly, waiting, expecting something, but not knowing what. Finally, when the wick had flickered out, she had given up and thrown herself down onto the pallet in the corner. Even then she had lain awake for hours, going over and over in her mind what had happened. From one day to the next—so quickly—her whole world had been overturned. And her father—what was happening to him? At last she had fallen into a restless sleep, but it seemed only a very short time until the cocks' crowing awakened her.

A hesitant knock at the door startled her. It opened, and the young nun who had brought her the food the afternoon before came in. She carried another bowl of gruel in her hands, with lumps of sodden bread floating on top. Her eyes were downcast; she wouldn't look at Ursula.

"What's happening? How long am I to be kept in here?" Ursula deliberately made her voice harsh. Although she was afraid, no one was going to know it.

The nun didn't answer. Before Ursula could question her further, she slipped back out the door, closing it behind her. Ursula heard the sound of a bar being dropped across it.

As the day progressed, a small amount of light found its way in through cracks and gaps in the walls near the roof. At first Ursula resumed her pacing. Frantic with fear and impatience, she stared at the door, willing it to open and let in somebody—anybody—who would tell her what was happening. The waiting—the not knowing—was unbearable. But the hours passed, and no one came. Finally, she threw herself down onto the pallet and buried her face in her arms, trying to block out what was happening, trying to make her mind blank, wanting to stop the images, each more horrible than the one before. They burned witches. Surely they couldn't really believe she was a witch. Surely they couldn't prove it.

The straw stank, and it was filled with fleas. Ursula leaped back up, scratching furiously at the bugs and the red welts that were coming up all over, until her skin was raw and bleeding. She started pacing again. She began to think she might go mad.

At the very moment when she could stand it no longer and had flung herself at the door, beating on it frantically, the bells of Cologne's churches began to peal. The bells of St. Maria's joined in, right over Ursula's head. The noise was horrendous. She clapped her hands over her ears, wincing with the pain of it, and huddled back into the farthest corner of the room.

It was two days before she saw anyone except the

nuns who attended to her needs. In all that time, not one of them uttered a word. Ursula had thought of escape. In her desperation she had dwelled on the possibility of overpowering the young nun who came in the mornings. It would be easy, but it was unthinkable to strike a nun. That would damn her for certain. And if she did manage to get out of the church, where would she go? Where could she hide? Her father was ill, and she had no way of knowing how he fared or even where he was. No one else in this city would take her in except possibly Bruno, and she would not put him in such danger.

On the third day, at the break of dawn, the light tap came at her door as usual. Ursula hardly bothered to look up. She was startled into awareness, however, by a stern male voice.

"You are to come with me now." A monk was standing behind the nun.

Ursula leaped to her feet. "Where are we going? What is to happen?"

"You are not to question. Just come with me."

At last! Was she to be released? She dusted herself off as best as she could and followed the monk out the door.

The brilliant sunlight outside struck her painfully. She threw a hand over her eyes to shield them and stumbled over the cobblestoned courtyard. The monk strode briskly ahead of her, forcing her to trot blindly to keep up. As her eyes grew accustomed to the light, she realized they were heading toward Great St.

Martin's. A cold knife of fear suddenly twisted inside her chest. It was in the courtyard at St. Martin's that criminals were tried and sentences handed out. It was in the courtyard of St. Martin's that witches were burned.

As Ursula struggled to keep up, she realized just how filthy she was. The hand shading her eyes was encrusted with dirt. The woolen shift she was wearing was stained and reeked with the smell of her own unwashed body. Her fair hair was matted, dark, and greasy. She, who had despised most of her neighbors for their uncleanliness and their stink, now stank worse than any of them. She dropped her hand from her eyes and began to run her fingers through the mess that was her hair, trying fruitlessly to tidy it. She brushed, uselessly, at the dirt on her shift.

By the time they reached St. Martin's, she was exhausted and panting. Three days of imprisonment with very little food had weakened her more than she would have thought possible. When the monk suddenly stopped, she almost ran into him. He stepped aside distastefully. Ursula looked up and saw what waited for her beyond him.

The courtyard was thronged with people. The noise of their excited voices rose in a tremendous swell as they caught sight of her. She stared around, trying to find a familiar face, but, in her shock, she couldn't make out one from another. Then her eyes were drawn to the far end of the courtyard. There, seated behind long trestle tables under the spreading branches of an ancient, red-leafed blood oak, were the monks of St. Martin's. The monk who had taken her from her house was seated almost in the middle, but what stunned Ursula to the point where she momentarily forgot to breathe was the sight of the figure sitting in the exact center: the archbishop of Cologne himself, resplendent with shards of sunlight glinting from the gold- and jewel-studded robe that fell around him. The archbishop of Cologne! He only judged the most serious cases of heresy. Frantically, Ursula looked around, desperate to see if there was anyone else to be judged here, but she stood alone.

"Step forward, my child." The archbishop's voice was kind, almost pitying, and for a moment Ursula felt hope.

The hope soon died. One after another, the townspeople rose to testify against her. Mistress Elke, recovered from childbirth and more virulent and poisonous than ever, was first.

"She cursed me! She said I carried a demon!"

In vain Ursula tried to deny it, but she was not allowed to speak.

Mistress Ingrid was quick to confirm it, swearing that she had heard the curse with her very own ears. Ursula knew that to be impossible, but by now the woman had fully convinced herself of the truth of what she was saying and she believed it implicitly.

"She turned herself into a cat. Only a witch can do that," Mistress Elke ranted on. She was flushed and sweating. The day was warm and her weight, in addition to the weakness from the recent childbirth, was beginning to tell. She staggered and would have fallen if one of the bystanders had not rushed to bring her a stool.

Sympathetic murmurs for her obvious distress began to rise, while increasingly hostile glances were directed toward the bedraggled, filthy Ursula.

"I saw that." Mistress Elke's maidservant ran to fan her mistress and add her lies to the rest.

"That's not true! *Nothing* of what they're saying is true!"

"That's enough, girl. It is not for you to speak, except to beg God's forgiveness for your sins." The archbishop's tone was sharper now.

Others rose who had nothing specific to say, but who testified that Ursula was "prideful," or thought herself better than ordinary people.

"She boasted that she was a healer," said one. "A *healer!* How could a mere girl be a healer?"

"It was because of that book," said another. "She was always reading in that book."

"And how is it that she can read?"

With a sinking heart, Ursula recognized Britta. The girl's face was malevolent; she was obviously relishing the opportunity of taking revenge for past snubs, real and imagined. "I can't read," Britta went on. "None of us can. How can she? That's the devil's work, if you ask me!"

At this the monk stood up. He held Ursula's book of healing.

"Yes," he said. "The book. This book." He held it

up. "A book that belongs to the church of Great St. Martin's. Tell us, girl, how you came by it."

"Brother Bernhard gave it to me." Ursula's voice wavered in spite of herself.

The monk turned toward the archbishop. "This book, your worship, disappeared shortly before our poor brother's death. Brother Bernhard had been in failing health—both of body and of mind—before he died, and we were desperately worried about whose hands it might have fallen into." He turned back to Ursula. His voice rose. "We see now that a thieving, sneaking girl—a willing servant of the devil—took possession of it."

"He gave it to me! He recognized that I was a healer!"

A murmur broke out among the crowd.

"She admits it!"

"See—she does claim to be a healer!"

The monk silenced them with a wave of his hand. "What she says is impossible," he said. "Brother Bernhard would never willingly have given this book away. He was a devoted monk, a loyal member of our community. He knew that this book could be used for evil by the wrong persons."

"How could it be used for evil? It is a book of healing! A book that could only bring good—bring relief of suffering." Desperately, Ursula pleaded. "I even cured a dog with it. I mended a dog's broken leg. Who else has done that?" The words poured out in a torrent before she realized the danger.

"She used a holy book to cure a dog!" The murmurs became cries of shock.

"Blasphemy!"

"A witch indeed!"

The monk turned toward Ursula with a terrible look. "Even true and holy things," he thundered, "even true and holy things such as this book can become evil if they are obtained by evil means and if they are used for evil purposes."

The murmurs and shocked outbursts had now become a roar. The archbishop was forced to hold up his hands for silence.

Ursula heard the rest of the trial as if through a thick, smothering blanket. Every time she tried to speak she was silenced, sometimes with physical force. She gave up. She stood, head high, staring unseeing at the hard, implacable blue of the heavens above.

This has nothing to do with me, she thought defiantly. These are the ravings of a horde of insane people. It's not happening.

She ceased to listen. In her own mind, she even ceased to be there. The impossible words, when they came, struck her with a force that was stronger than any physical blow.

"Unfortunately, the evidence is not to be denied," the archbishop said. He stood and stretched his hands out to Ursula as if to bless her, but his next words were not a benediction. "The accused stands convicted. She is a witch. For the remission of her sins— for the salvation of her soul—she will be burned.

Confess, my child, and be forgiven in heaven. Praise be to God."

Only then did Ursula see her father in the crowd. He was standing in the church doorway, half supported by Bruno. His face was ashen. He looked like one already dead.

# Chapter 5

hey took Ursula back to her cell at St. Maria Lyskirchen. She was not allowed to speak to her father or Bruno. The door closed behind her; the bar thudded down. Ursula stood for a moment, staring at the wall in front of her. It was noon and she had not yet eaten, but she wasn't aware of hunger. She wasn't aware of anything except the archbishop's words: "She is a witch. She will be burned." The words repeated themselves over and over in her mind. They branded and consumed her thoughts, just as the fire that was to come would brand and consume her body.

For days no one came near the cell except the nuns and the monk, who visited her each morning to urge her to repent and confess her theft and witchcraft. Ursula would not speak to him. She lost track of the days. She lay on her pallet in the corner, turning her face to the wall whenever a nun came in and barely touched the food they left for her. She had never seen a burning, but she could imagine it. Whenever she drifted off into an uneasy sleep, she would suddenly awaken, screaming with the pain of the flames. Everything in her small cell became permeated with the smell of smoke, even with the taste of smoke, until finally she couldn't eat at all.

Then, one morning, the monk came accompanied by two others. Ursula braced herself for the usual ordeal, but this time it was not forthcoming. The monk seemed angry, and all he would say was a curt order: "Follow us."

Ursula rose, but she was too weak to stand unaided. She would have fallen if one of the nuns had not held her. It was the young nun who usually came in the morning. When Ursula leaned on her for support, she saw pity in the girl's eyes. In a flash, all of her pride returned. She tore herself away from the nun and, summoning strength that wasn't really there, she stood alone. When the monk led the way out of the cell, she brushed away the nun's hand and followed him. This time she didn't ask where they were going. She knew.

By the time they had traversed the long passageway of the cloisters and crossed the garden that lay beyond it, Ursula was staggering. She realized, with a sense of desperation, that she could not possibly walk all the way to the courtyard at Great St. Martin's, to where the stake was waiting for her—and the torch. But she would *not* be carried. She forced herself forward.

"Ursula!"

The cry startled her. She felt herself seized from behind, but before she could pull away, she recognized her father. Then another, stronger arm lent support to them both. Unbelievably, it was Bruno.

"What—? What is happening?" Ursula whispered. "Are you come to take me—to take me to—" She couldn't finish the sentence.

"We are taking you away. By the grace of God, you have been pardoned." Master William's voice was weak, and there were tears running down his cheeks, but he grasped her even more tightly.

"I don't understand." Ursula's brain was whirling. She had been preparing, with every shred of will remaining to her, to die.

"You have been pardoned," Bruno repeated. "It's true. Your father has arranged for your release."

"But how?"

"Don't talk now. You are too weak," Bruno said. "Just come with us, and after you have rested we'll explain."

For once in her life, Ursula was only too glad to obey.

She had expected them to take her back to her own house, half forgetting that it had burned down. Instead, they were directing their footsteps toward the Bishop's Church—the wealthiest sector of town, where the archbishop and the nobles lived in splendor. Ursula's mind took note of this, but she couldn't yet think clearly enough to question it. It was only when they turned in at the gate of the house of Count Emil himself that she finally balked.

"What are you doing? Why are we here?" she

asked, stopping and forcing them to stop with her. She stared at the massive stone building rising up in front of her—taller than any other house in all of Cologne. Like all the houses of the nobles, and even the Bishop's Church itself, this house had been built with stones taken from the ruins of the Romans' villas. It seemed to shimmer in the sunlight—white, with a dusky rose tinge. Ursula couldn't make sense of it. Was it just an apparition? Was this just a dream?

"Come, daughter. It's all right," her father said.

They led her through the gate, past the courtyard, and into the stables beyond. At the very end was a small hut. They took her into that. In the corner of it were two straw pallets, and Ursula sank onto one of them gratefully. A fire was burning against the back wall. The smell of a rich broth steamed out from a pot hung on a hook over it. The odor was so thick and so strong that for a moment Ursula's stomach turned, unable to cope with it. Then, as she lay back and closed her eyes, a familiar wet nose thrust itself into the palm of her hand.

"Samson!"

The dog burst into a frenzy of tail-wagging.

"Is he well, father?" For a moment Ursula's senses rushed back to her. "How does he?" Her hands searched for the wounded leg.

"He does marvelously well, daughter, but needs your ministering, I'm afraid. He wouldn't let me touch the bindings you put on him, much less change the poultice."

"I must—" Ursula began, trying to sit up.

"Not now. The leg is thriving; all swelling has gone. He has waited for you these past days; he can wait a little longer. And when you have slept and eaten, then I can tell you of the wondrous good thing that has befallen us, daughter. God has indeed been good to us. We have indeed been blessed." His tired old face was creased into a smile, and his eyes had a shine to them that Ursula had not seen for a long time.

Something wonderful must certainly have happened, Ursula thought. Then she caught sight of Bruno standing in the doorway. His face was set— worried and angry.

If what has happened is so wonderful, why looks he so troubled, Ursula thought, but she could reason no more. Her head dropped back onto the straw, and for the first time in days she slept soundly.

Ursula slept until it was dark. When she awoke, the smell of food no longer revolted her—in fact, she found she was almost starving. She ate all that her father gave her and then slept again.

When she next awoke, it was early morning and the cocks were crowing as usual. Her father brought her porridge, and again she ate eagerly. He had heated water, too, and she cleansed herself and washed her hair gratefully. She knew that her father and she were considered odd because of their obsession with cleanliness—many people thought them mad to expose themselves to the risks involved in wetting themselves so often. Nevertheless, once the filth and dirt had been removed, and her long, thick blond hair combed and tied neatly back, she felt as if she was coming back to life again. Her father had even managed to find her a clean shift from somewhere. Samson watched her curiously. He obviously shared the others' opinion of baths and took care not to get too close. As soon as she was finished, Ursula tended to him. That he didn't mind.

His leg was healing well. "Evil to cure a dog," she muttered as she worked. "Witchcraft. Work of the devil! Are not the poor simple beasts also living creatures?" With the return of her spirits, her pride and her anger had come back tenfold. As she finished with the dog, her father, who had gone out to buy food for their noon meal, returned. She turned to him eagerly, anxious now to have her questions answered. How had he saved her? What were they doing here under the auspices of Count Emil?

"Father—" she began, but he forestalled her.

"I know. I know. You have a thousand questions. Sit quietly now, and I shall tell you what has happened."

Ursula tied the last of the bindings into place and curled herself up beside the dog on a mat in front of the hearth.

"When they took you away," her father began, "I was so overcome with fear—with the shock of it all—that I swooned. I failed you there, daughter."

"No, father," Ursula interrupted quickly, "you didn't fail me!"

"I did," he repeated quietly. "When I came to my senses, I found myself in Mistress Ingrid's house, and that kindly woman was tending to me."

Ursula's eyebrows shot up at the word *kindly*. Her father seemed to have forgotten Mistress Ingrid's part in her trial, but she would not bring it up now. It was probably better that her father forget as much as possible of that horror.

"Bruno was there as well and eager to do all in his power to help. At first we couldn't find out where they had taken you, but then Bruno managed to learn that you were at St. Maria's. We asked permission to see you but were denied. All we were told was that you were to be tried as a witch. We attended the trial. . . . By then I was very ill. Without good Bruno I fear I would have collapsed entirely. And then . . . when the archbishop announced that you were to burn . . ." The old man stopped, his voice choked. He dropped his head and passed a hand over his eyes. "The trial itself is only a haze in my mind—I was so ill—but the archbishop's words . . . Those words I remember. Those words I will never forget."

"I saw you there, father, and I feared so for you. But how, then . . . How did you secure my release?"

Her father shook his head to clear it and looked back at her. He continued. "I couldn't move from the spot where I heard the sentence passed. All the folk went away about their own business. No one was left but Bruno. He tried to get me to leave, to go with him, but I was incapable of it. And then, suddenly, a man stood before me. He was dressed in the livery of one of Count Emil's servants. He addressed me very respectfully and told me the count wished to speak with me. He bade me follow him. I didn't think I would be able to, but again, with Bruno's help, I did. When we arrived here, I was ushered into the house, and the count himself received me in a large, magnificent hall. It was so splendid, Ursula, my child. So splendid . . ." His voice trailed off with the memory of it.

"Go *on*, father," Ursula urged impatiently.

Master William came back to his story. "Well, what happened, daughter, was that the count's good doctor had been taken with the pestilence and died, God rest his soul. But the count is making plans to go on the Crusade with the godly Peter the Hermit, who has been preaching here these last weeks. He has need of someone who has knowledge of herbs and healing to accompany him, and he has asked me. He has asked *me*, daughter, to accompany him on the Crusade!" He stopped once more, and his eyes were shining again. "Is it not a miracle?"

Ursula stared at her father, too stricken to speak. An icy coldness was working its way up her spine.

"And this is the truly wonderful part, Ursula," Master William went on, unaware of her reaction. "Do you remember the Hermit saying the pope has promised absolution of sins to all who go on the Crusade? Well, then, the count went to the archbishop, and the archbishop will give you a pardon if you go with us, under my care, and take part in the holy quest to free

Jerusalem from the infidels. My beloved child, we are to go together to the Holy Land! We are to go together to the Crusade, and you will be pardoned all your sins!"

Ursula found her voice. "But Count Emil, father!" she burst out. "You cannot serve him. He is an evil man. He has brought untold misery to the people of this town. He helped the Crusaders kill David's family!"

"I cannot believe that." Master William's face took on a stubborn look. "Bruno is a good boy and has helped me immeasurably, but I am certain he was wrong about that. Even if he were right, Count Emil is going on the Crusade, my daughter. The Crusade will cleanse him of his sins, too, as it will cleanse us of our sins to accompany him."

"I am guilty of no such sins as he," Ursula shot back. "I was unjustly accused!"

"Nevertheless, you were convicted. You were declared guilty of witchcraft by our own archbishop. If it was not for Count Emil, you would this very day be facing the stake."

"I cannot go with that man! I will not! I'd rather—" Ursula stopped. Rather die, she had been going to say. But would she? The memory of the last few days rose bitterly into her mind. All at once she could smell the smoke again, taste it.

A knock interrupted them. Bruno peered in through the doorway. Ursula leaped to her feet, and Samson trotted over to greet him.

"Bruno! Have you heard—? But of course you have."

"About the Crusade? Yes," Bruno said, but there was no enthusiasm in his voice. He reached out both hands to Ursula. "I would that there had been some other way of saving you."

The next day Ursula's father started fussing the moment she awoke. He had been summoned to Count Emil and ordered to bring Ursula with him. It seemed that the count wanted to see this "witch" himself. Ursula was none too pleased with the tone of the message, but there was nothing to do but obey.

"We are invited to break fast with the count," Master William said. "It is a great honor. Do hurry, daughter, and make yourself presentable." The main meal of the morning would be just before midday.

When they were ready, they left the hut and walked toward the front entrance of the great house. Ursula steeled herself not to feel intimidated, but that was impossible. The size of the house alone was enough to frighten the boldest of people. She had no idea at all what awaited her inside.

They were stopped at the door by a suspicious servant, but after giving their names, they were led into an enormous dining hall. Ursula tried not to gape, although the magnificence around her was hard to ignore. Even the entrance to the hall was huge. Massive stone pillars rose on either side of them, and intricate mosaic tiling—reminiscent of the Roman villas from which the building materials had been scavenged—covered the floor. As the servant spoke to them, his voice echoed in spite of the tapestries and hangings that covered the walls.

The dining hall itself was even more grand. At one end stretched a long trestle table. Ursula could see the count and his lady seated there, with lesser nobles and friends on either side of him. Other long tables filled the room. As they entered, the count glanced up. He signaled them to draw near.

Master William swept off his cloth cap and held it in front of him as he approached the table. He seemed to shrink into himself as he got closer.

I am not frightened, Ursula thought defiantly. She held herself as tall as she could and walked with a steady step toward the count, chin high in the air. But, in spite of herself, she flushed as she realized that the people in the crowd around them were whispering, nudging each other, and pointing at them.

Even when sitting, the count gave an impression of dangerous strength. His hair was silvery gray, and he wore it long. His hands played constantly with the knife on the table in front of him. He seemed to be holding himself in—holding an immense reserve of energy in check. Ursula almost imagined him tensed to spring at any moment. It was his eyes, however, that caught her. They were a very pale blue, almost gray, and they fixed on Ursula with a peculiar intensity.

"My lord," Master William said with a small bow, "you do us great honor."

"So this is your daughter, then?" the count answered, never taking those eyes from Ursula's face.

It took every bit of Ursula's willpower not to drop her own.

"Draw near, girl."

Ursula stood her ground defiantly. Her father turned, flustered, and would have pushed her forward, but Ursula stood fast.

"I said, draw near. I would inspect more closely the witch who is to accompany us on our holy Crusade."

Ursula's hands clenched. She drew a deep breath. "I am no witch."

There was a gasp throughout the room. The stuffing and cramming of food into mouths ceased momentarily.

"You were tried and sentenced by the archbishop himself," the count answered smoothly. "Do you dare dispute the findings of the church? The church that, in its mercy, has allowed you the opportunity to redeem your sins?"

"I dispute nothing, but I know I am not a witch. I am a healer."

The gasp grew into a murmur that swept through the room. The count frowned.

"Master William, it seems your daughter has learned nothing. Witch or not, the sin of pride spews out with every word she utters. Might it be I have erred in offering this salvation to her?" Although he spoke to her father, he stared still at Ursula.

Ursula's father clutched her arm. "Forgive her, my

lord. She is dazed. She knows not what she is saying. The events of the last few days . . . The fear she has suffered . . ."

"Fear? I see little evidence this girl has suffered much from fear," the count answered. His voice was silken but cold. "Perhaps God in his wisdom will remedy that." For a moment longer he held Ursula's eyes with his own. That there was a battle going on here Ursula had no doubt, but even if it was a battle she could not possibly win, she would not give in.

Then, with a bored wave of his hand, he dismissed her and turned to her father. He indicated a seat at the bottom of a nearby table. "Eat now," he said.

By the time they sat down, the platters and bowls of food had been thoroughly picked over. Slices of stale bread were passed to them to use as plates. A bowl full of greasy broth, with a few unwanted lumps of fatty meat, was presented to them. Master William dipped in with his fingers and captured one lump. Then, seeing that Ursula was not following his example, he procured another slab for her and put it on her bread.

"Eat, child. You must not insult our host."

Ursula made no move to pick it up. "I do not eat leftovers at anyone's table, father," she said contemptuously, but, although the food was less than appetizing, in truth her stomach was again knotted so tightly that eating would have been impossible.

That man is as evil as I believed, she thought bleakly. Perhaps even worse. What is to come of this?

The conversation, which had ceased when they sat down, began to flow again around them. No one addressed them directly. A few even edged discreetly away from them. If it had not been for her father, Ursula would have thrown her portion of food to the dogs that lurked under the tables and left.

It was late afternoon before they could get away and return to the stables. There they found everything bustling. The news had come that Peter the Hermit had determined to leave on the twenty-sixth of this month, April. Barely a week away! All must be made ready immediately.

For the next few days Ursula had little time to worry. All the herbs and ointments that had been in their home had been lost in the fire, but the garden was untouched. She and her father gathered as much as they could, then scoured the hills and the fields around for whatever else they could harvest. It was the wrong time of year for picking plants that should be gathered in full bloom, but they had been given a horse-drawn wagon by the count, and they transplanted many seedlings into boxes that could be stowed in it. With luck, some of them would flourish. On the last day at their house, Mistress Ingrid hovered around them like a pestering wasp.

"I'll look after things here until you return, don't you worry," she assured Master William, ignoring Ursula.

I'm sure she will, Ursula thought sourly. She'll be

picking through the ruins for what she can steal the moment our backs have disappeared down the street—if she hasn't already. Ursula tried to find the tabby cat, but there had been no sign of it since the fire, her father said, so she supposed it had found another source of milk. Fickle creature. But still, she reasoned, no different from anyone or anything else.

As they led the horse and herb-laden wagon up the street, Ursula turned for one last look at the rubble that used to be her home. When would she see it again? Would she ever see it again? The folk around the count's house were talking as if Jerusalem were but a month's trek away. A month's trek, a few weeks to chase out the Turks, and then, for those who chose to return, home again. Home by harvesttime for certain, secure in the knowledge that they had done God's will and God had forgiven them all their sins. And for those who had no home to return to, the promise of lands and properties such as they would never own here.

It could not be that easy, Ursula thought warily. But she said nothing. No one spoke to her, anyway.

All was ready. The wagon was loaded on the evening before the day set for their departure. Master William tended to the last-minute details in such a fluster of agitation that he nearly drove Ursula mad.

"Generous beyond all bounds, the count has been," he kept assuring her. "He has given us provisions enough for a year, a fine cart, a horse! And I will have a sack of coins to pay me for my services. Silver coins!

Enough to rebuild and set me up in my own business again when we return."

Finally, Ursula exploded. "Coins! I have seen no coins! I'll believe that when I see them."

Her father fell silent. The stubborn look she was beginning to know too well stole over his face again. "I cannot discuss this now. I have things to see to," he muttered and left.

Alone save for Samson, Ursula stared morosely into the fire until a rustling at the doorway startled her. It was Bruno.

"May I enter? I have come to bid you farewell."

At his words Ursula's heart sank even lower. "You have not changed your mind, then."

"You know I cannot join you," he answered quietly. "This Crusade goes against everything I have ever believed as a Christian. There will be killing. Fighting and killing. In spite of what your father says, I cannot believe that to be right. I would to God there had been some other way to save you."

Ursula poked at the embers without answering. They had been through this many times since her release. She could not argue with him.

Bruno threw himself down beside her. Samson crawled up to him, and he scratched the dog absent-mindedly behind the ears. "Where is your father?" he asked.

"He is off on some business of his own," she replied. "He is so happy—so full of joy. He has convinced himself this will be a truly marvelous venture."

They fell silent.

* * *

For a long time after Bruno left, Ursula remained by the fire. When the last embers finally died, she made no move to rekindle them. She was still there when her father returned.

"All is in readiness, daughter," he pronounced. "Tomorrow! Tomorrow we go on God's journey!" He curled up on his pallet in the corner, and his snores soon attested to the fact that, in spite of his excitement, he was asleep.

Ursula sat on. In the darkness Samson whimpered.

# Chapter 6

They were to meet by the river, outside the south wall of the city. Ursula and her father were up before dawn to feed the horse and finish loading the wagon. When they were done and had harnessed the horse to it, Ursula lifted Samson and settled him into a kind of nest she had made for him from some old mats right behind where she and her father would sit. Sacks of flour, bags of vegetables, oats for the horse, a quantity of other supplies, and their boxes of herbs took up most of the room. The wagon had no cover; but the count had also given them a sturdy tent; it occupied what little space was left over. Master William had been right on one account—the count had provided for them well.

"You had better ride until that leg has finished healing, my friend," Ursula said as she settled the animal down.

Beside the dog, two chickens squawked and flustered in a small wooden crate. Samson looked at them dubiously. Ursula took her place, her father gathered up the reins, and they were off. Neither Ursula nor her father had ever driven a wagon before, but the horse seemed to know what to do, so, except for guiding him where necessary, they left things up to him. He was plodding but willing. Ursula's father's eyes were bright, and he was still gripped with the excitement of the night before, but with every step the horse took, Ursula's heart grew heavier. They were leaving the only home she had ever known. There was no place for her there now, but she could only think with dread of what might lie ahead.

She had known that many people were expected to join the Hermit, but even so she drew in a breath of astonishment when they passed through the Korn Gate and saw the multitude crowding the field below the city. There must have been thousands. Everything was in complete confusion. Nobles and their attendant soldiers milled around on horseback, shouting commands; carts and wagons were attempting to line up in some kind of order but with no apparent success. Cattle, terrified and lowing, were adding to the confusion. Donkeys brayed. As if the noise was not already enough, the bells began to peal for the morning prayers. Ursula and her father drew in at the edge and waited, wondering what to do. No one seemed to be in charge; no one seemed to be trying to impose any kind of order whatsoever.

Suddenly a cheer went up from those closest to the

city walls. Peter appeared on his donkey. The cheer was picked up and echoed by the throng of people gathered there. A group of horsemen more splendidly garbed than the others, and armored in mail and leather jerkins, rode to meet him. Ursula recognized Count Emil. He and the other nobles formed a guard around the Hermit; their followers kept the crowd back. Peter surveyed the people gathered in the fields below him in the early morning dawn and stretched out his arms to them in blessing. He spoke a few words, but Ursula could not hear him. As the sun rose and the bells of Cologne pealed, priests passed through the horde of people. Mass was said. Ursula bowed her head to add her prayers to the rest, but words wouldn't come. For what should she pray? Success on their Crusade? Success would mean war and killing. The thought brought Bruno's face into her mind, and she felt a pang of real, physical pain. He had become more than a friend to her in these last few days—would she ever see him again?

Whips cracked, curses split the air, and the Crusade was on the move.

Peter and his guard of nobles led the way, followed by the other knights and their men. Foot soldiers fell in behind them, carrying long-handled halberds, their tips—half axe, half spear—reflecting bright splinters of light. Behind them came crossbowmen and archers armed with longbows. While all this was going on, the rest of the vast mass began to push and rush for their own positions. The Hermit and his guard swung off down the path that followed the river southward and soon disappeared from view, leaving chaos in their wake.

"Father, let us wait a few moments." It was with difficulty that Ursula restrained Master William from adding the crack of his whip to the others and plunging into the melee. "There is such confusion, surely it would be wise to tarry until it sorts itself out before we try to join. Besides," she added, "we have not had a morsel to eat this morning. Here, take this." She handed him some bread and cheese from a packet she had placed on the seat beside her.

Master William allowed himself to be persuaded, but it was with obvious impatience that he nibbled at the food—hardly tasting it in his excitement. Ursula watched his flushed face with concern. Such agitation could not be good for him.

Even Samson was restless. He whined with eagerness to be let loose to investigate all the new smells that were filling the air around him. Ursula tossed him a piece of bread to quiet him. As she was doing so, a loud crash startled her. She looked up to see that two wagons had collided. The wheel of one spun off, and the wagon collapsed onto the ground. The owner leaped to accost the owner of the offending wagon, and in the next second they had come to blows. Other wagons hurried to maneuver around them and take their places.

Finally, after the greater number of the wagons had managed to set off, Ursula could restrain her father no longer, and they managed to ease their way in. At the end of the procession straggled those who must make the journey on foot: hundreds of men, women, and children, some of them driving a thin cow or scrawny donkey, all laden down with bundles and provisions. Behind them, all the bells of Cologne pealed joyously.

They followed the river, keeping on the western side where the land was flatter. On the opposite side, the heavily forested hills rose straight up from the riverbanks, becoming steeper and steeper as they progressed. Ursula had lived beside this river all her life and had taken it for granted, but now at every bend it surprised her anew. The floods of spring were in full flow, and the river widened unexpectedly in places to such an extent that it looked more like an inland sea—but not a calm sea. The current ripped toward them with an almost unbelievable speed and power, carrying branches, even whole trees in its grip. Any person or animal who fell into that fury would be swept away instantly.

They forged steadily on during the day, but even with all their enthusiasm, the people on foot dropped farther and farther behind. Finally, in the late afternoon, they rounded yet another curve in the path and saw stretched before them an immense plain. The leaders had stopped here, and already tents were mushrooming up almost as far as the eye could see. The tents of the nobility were easy to pick out. Gathered at the farthest end of the plain, they were brilliantly colored, with streamers and pennants flying bravely from their poles. The red cross of the Crusade was very much in evidence. The tents of the rest of the folk were drab and plain in comparison—in some cases no more than a cloth stretched between two poles—but on them, too, the flaming cross had been defiantly stitched or painted. Fires were springing up all over the encampment, the smells of food cooking were beginning to waft out, and the people were coming to life after a long day of unaccustomed journeying.

Ursula helped her father unload their tent. Samson, delighted to be on the ground again, trotted stiffly around them in circles for a while and then was off to explore the new surroundings. Together, but with much difficulty, Ursula and Master William managed to erect their tent. They had straw to strew over the ground inside and rugs to throw over that. When they were finished, it looked snug and comfortable. Ursula began to feel a little easier. The small, familiar chores of beginning the evening meal, even though being done in such strange surroundings, comforted her somewhat.

"I must go to Count Emil and see what his wishes are," Master William said then.

"Can you not rest first, father?" Ursula objected. "It has been a tiring day for you."

"No, child. I must do my duty to the count before all else. I'll return as soon as possible."

Ursula watched as he walked toward the count's encampment. In spite of his weariness, there was a spring to her father's step that she had not seen in a long time. A small hope stirred within her.

Perhaps, she thought, perhaps good will come of this pilgrimage for us after all.

She gathered sticks for a fire. Then she walked to the river to a spot where the banks formed a kind of sheltered inlet and dipped a kettle in for water. Several other women were there before her. She would have greeted them, but as soon as she appeared, one whom she recognized began whispering excitedly to another. Ursula could not hear what was being said, but the finger pointing at her and the shocked expression of the women told her all she needed to know. It seemed that her reputation was following her along here, too. Cheeks flaming, she tossed her hair away from her face and strode angrily out of the clearing.

Samson greeted her as she returned to their campsite, almost frisky in spite of his injured leg. To her surprise, a large, red-faced man was standing beside their tent. He carried a shovel held out in front of him, and in it were smoking coals. Ursula stopped, hesitant.

"There are those of us with good wagons who are charged with carrying coals and seeing that they do not go out. I have brought you some," he said.

Reassured, Ursula smiled gratefully. Starting a fire was always difficult, and she was not handy with flints and tinder.

"I thank you," she said.

The man tossed his smoldering coals into the middle of the small pile of sticks that Ursula had gathered. They caught immediately and flared up in a satisfying blaze.

"That is very kind of you—" Ursula began, but the man cut her short.

"And now, if you please, mistress, you will give me two copper coins."

"What?" Ursula's mouth dropped open. "I have no coins! I thought the fire was a gift, neighborly help."

The man laughed coarsely. "And pigs fly themselves right into the dinner pot! Pay up, my girl. You get nothing in this life for free."

"But I have no coins. Really! My father might have a few, but he is not here." As soon as the words were out of her mouth, she regretted them.

"Oh, alone, are you? And no coins? Perhaps we should barter, then. Now let's see— What might you have that you could exchange for the gift I've given you?" The man leered and thrust his face close to hers.

Ursula jumped back, but he grabbed her arm and pulled her close to him.

"Let me go!" she commanded. "Take your hands off me at once!" She tried to break away, but he held her fast.

"Gratitude, my girl. When a man gives a wench a gift, he can expect a little satisfaction."

Ursula's mind raced. She and her father, seeking

privacy, had deliberately made their camp away from the rest—there was no one immediately near. A few others, who were possibly within earshot, seemed to be deliberately ignoring the whole situation. Ursula let herself go limp for a moment. Then when the man's grip on her arm relaxed, she tore herself free. She scooped up the shovel, which he had dropped, swung it, and caught him below the knees. He howled with pain and crumpled to the ground. In the next instant he leaped back up and advanced on her with murderous hate in his eyes.

"So," he hissed. "That's how you would like to play, is it?"

Ursula held the shovel in front of her. He was much bigger and stronger than she, but she was no weakling, and with a heavy shovel for a weapon she could well defend herself. At that moment Samson decided to join the fray. He put himself in between Ursula and the man and growled. The man stepped quickly back out of reach of shovel and dog.

"Pah!" he spat. "I have no time for the likes of you. If you really have no coins, then you'll have to give me something else." He strode over to the wagon and seized the box containing the chickens. "This should do. Now I'll have my shovel as well, if it pleases you, wench."

"You can't have those! Your miserable coals aren't worth half of one of them!" Ursula raised the shovel once more, prepared to do battle all over again. Samson took two stiff-legged steps forward, but his attention was now distracted by the box of frantically clucking chickens. Taking advantage of the moment, the man snaked out his free hand and grabbed the shovel. Ursula was caught off guard and lost her balance. Before she knew what had happened, she was sprawled full length on the dusty ground and the man was striding off. She stared after him with fury and brushed away Samson's inquiring nose. If she had been a witch, the man would have been one of his own burning cinders before he could have taken another step.

She was sitting by the fire that had been purchased at such a high price, tending a stew that was bubbling away over it, when her father returned.

"Splendid fire, Ursula," he remarked cheerfully. "I was afraid you wouldn't be able to get it going. Well done, daughter."

Ursula remained grimly silent. There would be time enough later to tell him about the chickens.

Darkness fell soon after they had eaten. Torches were lit; their flames quickly dotted the plain around them and all up and down the riverbank. Across the river, the silhouette of a solitary, wall-encircled keep, high atop a steep cliff, showed black against the last faint vestiges of the day's light. Torches sprang up within it, too. Ursula stared at it and wondered what manner of people moved about within. A voice spoke at her shoulder.

"There be dragons over there, so they say."

Ursula started. It was an old woman, on her way

back from the river to her own camping spot. At that moment a long, eerie, ululating howl throbbed across the water. It was repeated, then picked up and echoed once, then again, and then yet again.

Dragons there might or might not be, Ursula thought with a shudder, but wolves there certainly were.

When Ursula crawled out of their tent the next morning, she was enveloped in a world of white. Thick fog hung over the ground they were camped on. The river itself was invisible. All the normal morning sounds of the awakening camp were muffled and far away; she and her father could have been totally alone. She groped her way down to the bank to fetch water. The cold smell of the blanketed river hung heavy and dank in the air.

The fire had gone out. Ursula managed to get it going again after a great deal of trouble. She then boiled the water and made a thick porridge. The warm food was welcome, and she drew her cloak tightly around her against the early morning dampness.

By the time they had finished eating, the mist had started to clear along the riverbank, although the river itself was still enshrouded. They joined the others for the morning mass and then struck camp and took their place at the end of the train of wagons.

They rode in silence. Ursula felt as if the fog weighing down on the river and the hills opposite was weighing down on her just as heavily. Her emotions felt blanketed as well—almost numb. Not one person had bade them a good morning, and she fancied that conversations stopped when they approached. It might have been her imagination, but she thought not. It seemed that God might be willing to pardon her, but her companions on this Crusade were not. She sat straighter in her seat, chin held high, and set herself to ignoring them. If that was the way they wanted it, so be it. She had no need of *them*.

After a time the mist on the river began to lift. Gradually, Ursula could begin to see the outlines of the hills on the other side. The forests emerged as if coming to life after an evil spell. A shaft of sun broke through from behind one steep slope, and then fingers of light seemed to play with the gauzy haze. Shreds of vapor tore, parted, and tried to join together again in vain. The sun, at first dull and indistinct, finally emerged in a triumphant blaze. Within minutes, it seemed, the rest of the mist disappeared. A few minutes more and it was warm enough to loosen her heavy cloak. The sun and the warmth did nothing, however, to lighten her spirits.

For three days they followed the river while the hills on the other side grew higher, and the river itself narrowed until all of its might was channeled into a rock-strewn, swift-running gorge. The first goal of this journey was the city of Mainz, but as they drew nearer to it, disturbing rumors began to fly back and forth. A large party of Crusaders had preceded them along the river—there were tales of disaster and more killings of Jews.

"Every Jew in Trier was slaughtered," one man told Master William and insisted on it in the face of the old man's horrified objections. "It's God's truth. There's not one of them left."

Finally, the walls of Mainz loomed in the distance. An ominous pall of smoke hung over it. They set up camp earlier than usual beside the river. Ursula had become more adept at lighting fires by now, and to her relief the man who had threatened her on their first night out had not reappeared. It was still light when they finished their evening meal; she hurried to tidy up.

"Why such haste, daughter?" her father asked querulously. Master William's initial excitement had given way to fatigue by now, and the rigors of such constant travel were beginning to show. He looked tired and ill. Added to that, the count had been indisposed on the last two nights and had sent for him several times. Ursula didn't think that her father had managed more than a few hours' sleep either night.

"I'm going to see what the talk in the camp is, father," Ursula replied. "There have been so many stories—now that we're on the outskirts of Mainz, perhaps someone will be able to tell me what the truth of the matter is. You should try to sleep," she added. "You said the count was better last night—we can hope he won't call you tonight."

Not quite knowing what she intended to do, Ursula made her way toward the encampment of the Hermit and the nobles. As she drew near, a woman hurried out of one of the tents carrying an armload of pots and kettles. Ursula hesitated, unwilling to speak and risk yet more scorn, but the woman was a stranger and fear for the fate of David and the rest of his family finally gave her the courage to approach.

"Good evening," she said, bracing for a rebuff, but the woman looked at her without interest or recognition, obviously more anxious to get on with her chores than to talk.

"I've been hearing stories," Ursula began. "Rumors that there have been fighting and killing in the cities. Have you heard anything?"

The woman stopped and looked at Ursula more closely. "The Jews," she said, nodding. "They have been killing the Jews again. It's an odd way to do Christ's work, it seems to me."

"What happened?" Ursula asked, her voice shaking.

The woman nodded toward the walls of Mainz, where the smoke still rose thick and black. "They tried to hide in their temple, and the Crusaders set it on fire."

"How many—?" Ursula began, but the woman dropped her eyes.

"It's not for me to be talking of such things. The good Peter will tell us what we need to know." She averted her head, clutched her pots to her, and scurried away.

"Nearly every one," a voice behind Ursula said. "Out of eight hundred Jews in Mainz, they say there is only a handful left."

Ursula whirled around with a gasp. Standing in front of her, disheveled and exhausted, stood Bruno.

# Chapter 7

The shock of seeing Bruno was so great that for a moment Ursula couldn't find her voice. Finally, she managed to speak.

"Bruno! What are you doing here? How—?"

"It seems I couldn't let you go off on your own after all," he answered. He rubbed at his forehead slowly. "I stood and watched you from the city gate on the morning you left and I almost ran after you then, but I couldn't go without speaking to my master at the church. I tried very hard all that day to convince myself that my place was in Cologne, not on this Crusade. I tried the next day as well, but somehow or other, when I went to work that morning, I found myself asking if I could be excused. The work on the church is nearly done, and my master thinks the Crusade is a worthwhile and godly venture, so he let me go. I followed as quickly as I could, only stopping for a few hours' sleep when I had to, and here I am."

The weight that had bowed Ursula down disappeared. She felt suddenly light-headed—almost giddy. "I am so glad to see you!" she cried. Then his first words sank in. "But the Jews? What did you say about the Jews of Mainz? Surely you were mistaken."

"I wish with all my heart that I were," Bruno answered. "But I have the information from one who witnessed it all. There are eight to ten Jews left in Mainz at the most."

"David?" Ursula whispered. "What about David?"

Bruno shrugged hopelessly. "There's no way of knowing. Those who escaped are being well hidden. No one will speak of them."

Samson trotted over at that moment. Bruno reached down to pat him, the look of pain on his face deepening. At the sight of the dog, Ursula's eyes filled with tears. She knelt quickly and buried her face in his scraggly fur, the weight and the worry returning. But the touch of Bruno's hand on her shoulder brought a measure of comfort.

Thank God that he has come, she thought. With Bruno here now, perhaps this can be borne.

Finally, the Crusaders reached the point where they had to cross the Rhine and leave the Rhine Valley. From here they would make their way up the Neckar River until they reached the waters of the almost legendary Danube River. The Danube would lead them the gentlest way around the mountains that stood between them and the Byzantine Empire—mountains so high, it was said, that snow stayed on them all summer long.

At the crossing point, they camped on a wide plain; the people filled it as far as Ursula could see. A fleet of small wooden boats bobbed in the river current just offshore. She looked at them dubiously.

"Surely we are not meant to make such a dangerous crossing in those tiny craft," she said.

"They say they will bring larger ferries for the wagons and horses," Bruno answered, but he, too, looked worried.

They began early the next morning, but it was obvious that it would take days to ferry them all across. The current had abated a bit, but the crossings each took almost an hour and looked to be filled with danger. Just how dangerous they actually were was suddenly brought home to those watching on the shore. For some reason the oarsmen on one ferry faltered when they reached the middle—in the fastest and most treacherous part of the current. A shout went up from the boatman, but it was too late. In the instant that the oarsmen faltered, the current caught the boat and swung it broadside. Within seconds it veered, was swamped, and overturned. Before Ursula's horrified eyes, men, horses, and the boat itself were all carried out of sight around a bend.

"Go in one of the small boats with your father," Bruno urged when it was their turn. "They're safer. I'll go with the horse and wagon in the ferry."

"No," Ursula answered stubbornly. Afraid though

she was, she would not leave it up to Bruno to care for their belongings. "I'll stay with the wagon."

Master William would not be separated from them either, so together father and daughter braced themselves against the lurching seat of the wagon as Bruno guided it onto the ferry. Ursula fought down panic. She had never been off the land before, and the river that had seemed wide, even from the safety of the shore, was now unbelievably frightening. What she hadn't expected was the noise. The current hissed and sucked and slapped at the boat like a living thing. The oarsmen sweated with the strain of fighting their way across while the ferry rocked and lurched insanely. Water spewed over the low sides in a drenching spray. It seemed an eternity before they were safely on the other side.

As the horse and wagon lumbered off the ferry, Ursula leaped down onto the ground. Never before had she appreciated just how good it was to have firm earth beneath her feet. Samson seemed to feel the same way. He, too, jumped off at the first possible moment. Then, pointing his nose to the sky, he gave a couple of happy barks at nothing at all—just for the sheer joy of being a dog back on land again.

The hills along the Neckar sloped more gradually, and the forests were less deep. The land opened out a bit on either side of the river; the going was less rough. Ursula's father's spirits brightened perceptibly as they traveled on. The count had recovered from his indisposition, and Master William had been able to get his rest at night.

"Look at what marvelous distances we are marching each day, daughter," he declared. "We are getting closer and closer to Jerusalem all the time!"

But Ursula could not share his enthusiasm. Each day, the people on foot dragged farther and farther behind. She could not get the memory out of her mind of what they looked like, straggling into the camp hours after the wagons had arrived. The night before, she had been stirring their evening stew when a woman carrying a baby and leading another child by the hand shambled past their campsite. There seemed to be no man with them. The woman had stared at their well-provisioned wagon and their fire burning brightly against the night airs, and a look almost of hate had crossed her face. Ursula had been stricken. At first all she had been able to do was stare back. By the time she had collected herself enough to think of offering to share their food, the woman and her children had disappeared into the darkness. Ursula could not stop thinking about David, either. They had not been able to get any further news about him or his family, and now they were far past Mainz. It seemed likely that she would never know.

One night, just after they had made camp and Bruno had gone to collect firewood, he returned, breathless.

"Peter is to speak. Hurry—we should go to hear him."

Ursula jumped up and helped her father struggle to his feet beside her. Peter had not spoken to them at all since they had left. They hurried to the nobles' end of the campsite along with most of the others, hanging on tightly to each other so as not to get separated in the crush.

The Hermit's eyes burned with fervor. His voice rang out over the crowd, echoing Ursula's father's words as he rejoiced with them over the distance they had already traveled. He was even thinner than before—his emaciated frame looked as if it were being consumed from within by the same fire that flamed from his eyes.

"We will triumph!" he cried. "Our holy Crusade will set Jerusalem free for all time. The infidels will fall before our might like moths before a flame. God wills it!"

The nobles and the soldiers who flanked him drew their swords. For a moment the sound of iron being drawn drowned out everything else. Then they raised their weapons high in the torchlight, and their voices roared to join with the Hermit's.

"God wills it!" they cried. "God wills it!"

Ursula stole a sideways glance at Bruno. His face was as grim as it had been the very first morning he heard the Hermit preach. She felt a shiver of apprehension crawl down her spine. The mob that day had been frightening but, for the most part, unarmed. And murder had still been done. The spectacle that presented itself in the flickering glow of flames this night was much more frightening. She remembered how Bruno had argued against the Crusade then. And now, here he was. Because of her.

The majority of the people took the speech as a signal to celebrate. Barrels of ale were opened, and wineskins were passed around freely. By midnight most of the soldiers and a goodly part of the common people were drunk. Ursula sat at the open flap of their tent, holding herself away from the commotion. The count had sent for Master William after the carousing had begun to die down, and he had gone with his bags of herbs and medicines. Bruno had disappeared without a word.

What if he doesn't come back? The thought worried and teased at her. What if he has realized that he wants nothing to do with this after all and he's returned to Cologne? One part of her mind knew he would not go without telling her; the other part imagined the worst. When he finally did return and started to make up his bed under the wagon, she could not resist a sharp comment.

"I thought perhaps you had left us," she said.

Bruno looked up at her over the dying fire, surprised.

"You know I would do no such thing," he answered.

"You didn't want to come. The way the Crusaders are behaving tonight—"

"I like it not, that is true. I'm afraid of what is to come."

"I did not ask you to join us. It was your decision," Ursula burst out. She listened to her words with horror, but she was powerless to stop them. "It's not my fault that you are here!"

"Of course not. I have never said so." Bruno straightened up. "What is troubling you, Ursula?"

"Nothing," she answered shortly and retreated into the tent, pulling the flap shut behind her. It's not my fault, she repeated to herself. Nevertheless, she felt guilty. It was not a comfortable feeling.

"Father, our supplies are dwindling," Ursula announced as Master William emerged from the tent early the next morning. In the cold light of dawn, his face looked pale and tired, the previous day's enthusiasm evaporated away. The count had kept him very late the night before.

"Child, we are well provided for," her father answered distractedly. "The wagon bursts at its seams."

"True," Ursula agreed. "But we are using things up more quickly than I had expected. Without the chickens we have no eggs, and there are weevils in the flour. Have you spoken to the count again about the bag of silver he promised us? I would feel easier if we had it."

"The count has promised to take care of us," Master William said. His manner was evasive. "He will see to our wants."

"But, father—he has promised! We should hold him to his word. He is so devious—I trust him not."

"This is not your concern, daughter," her father answered shortly. "The count and I have come to our arrangements. There is no need for you to worry."

"But—" Ursula's words were cut off as he turned irritably away from her.

"I have a few coins," Bruno said from behind her as her father walked away. "My master paid me before I left."

"You had better save those for yourself, seeing as you are so worried about how things are going to turn out," Ursula replied. Again, she regretted her harsh words the instant they were out of her mouth, but she had never accepted alms from anyone in her life and she had no intention of beginning now.

Bruno turned away without answering.

They got off to a slow start that day. More than half the company appeared to be suffering greatly from the effects of the night before. Pale, sweating men cursed wagons and beasts; accidents were more numerous than ever; and fights broke out in every quarter. It was almost noon before their wagon could move.

They passed through numerous villages on their way up the Neckar. Word of their coming had obviously gone ahead of them, and in every little town the people flocked out to see them, to wish them well, and even to press food and provisions on them.

"God speed you," one woman called out to Ursula as their wagon passed by. To Ursula's amazement, she was holding out a live chicken in offering.

For a moment Ursula was tempted; then her pride

reasserted itself. "Thank you, mistress, but we have no need of that."

"Weren't you worrying about supplies?" her father observed. "That chicken would have come in very handy."

"We have no need of charity, father," Ursula answered stiffly. "There are those who are in far greater want."

Her father sighed and watched regretfully as the woman in the wagon behind them accepted the chicken greedily.

The valley began to narrow and steepen. The Neckar was not nearly as big a river as the Rhine, and the hills on either side were nowhere near as high, but the land now rose sharply on both sides of the river. The Crusaders found themselves strung out in a long, narrow file. It was difficult in these circumstances to find a place large and wide enough for them to camp. At one village, however, the land flattened out to some extent into fields that the villagers had cultivated. The Hermit stopped there.

As Bruno and Ursula set up the tent and made the evening fire, the townspeople, curious about the Crusade and anxious to hear more about it, began to filter into the camp. Many of them brought gifts of food.

"Good even, mistress," a voice said hesitantly from the darkness at the edge of the firelight.

Ursula looked up to see a young boy staring at her shyly. For a moment he reminded her of David. She caught her breath. Then she saw he was holding out a handful of small, wizened turnips.

"We have not much, mistress, but what we have we would share with you who are on such a holy Crusade," he said.

An automatic refusal came to her lips but died as she looked into the boy's eyes.

"Thank you," she said, reaching out for the offering. "We thank you very much."

The boy beamed. "Go with God," he said and scampered away.

Ursula looked up and saw Bruno smiling for the first time in a long while. "The true spirit of God does show itself in unexpected places, doesn't it?" he said.

Unsure of what he meant, Ursula turned quickly to add the turnips to their stores.

That evening, just as they were finishing their meal, the sound of music drifted over to them from a circle of people gathered around a large fire in the middle of the camp. Ursula was immediately interested, Bruno as well. They had not heard music since they left Cologne.

"Shall we go over and see what is happening?" Bruno asked.

"Yes, let us," Ursula answered, surprised at the lightening and excitement in her heart. "Will you come, too, father?"

"No, child," the old man answered. "I will rest and listen from here."

Ursula looked at him, worried for a moment. He seemed very tired and frail, but Bruno reached out a hand and pulled her to her feet.

As they reached the fire, they saw four people

standing near it. There were three men and a woman. The men were dressed in brightly colored tunics and hoods; the woman wore a soft woolen shift of deep blue. In the flickering firelight, it set off her pale golden hair perfectly. Each was playing an instrument. One man, who seemed to be the leader of the group, was playing a lute. Another blew into an ocarina. The third man had a strange instrument that Ursula had never seen before. It consisted of a skin pouch, which he tucked under his arm, attached to a pipe, into which he blew. The music thus produced was wild and haunting, almost overpowering all the rest. The woman was beating time on a little drum hanging from her neck and decorated with many colored ribbons. She was singing, and her clear voice carried easily to where Ursula and Bruno stood. As they watched and listened, Ursula became aware that the woman was not as old as she had supposed. In fact, she looked to be only a few years older than Ursula herself—no more than a girl yet. Suddenly, Ursula was surprised to see a small face peek out from behind her skirts. The men joined in the singing. Ursula did not understand the words—they were in a dialect she had never heard before, but the tunes were at once lively and haunting and the voices exceptionally good. The woman's voice, in particular, was pure and true.

They sang and played for around an hour. Ursula sat beside Bruno on the grass, eyes closed, carried away from herself with the sweet music. She could almost believe she was back in Cologne, listening to a group of strolling minstrels in their own marketplace. When they finally stopped, she opened her eyes with a sigh of regret. Back to reality and to a field that was getting cold and damp.

The minstrels bowed low. Then the woman reached behind her and pulled forth a tiny girl. The child's fine hair hung down far below her narrow shoulders, paler even than the woman's—nearly white in the firelight. The woman whispered something in her ear and pushed her forward. Reluctantly, the child moved. She came hesitantly toward the group of people, holding out a tattered velvet pouch. Some people laughed and tousled her hair as they dropped a coin into her bag. She came toward Ursula.

"I have nothing for her," Ursula whispered.

"I have a small coin," Bruno answered.

The child approached them. Her eyes were wide, and she had the air of a wild fawn that if startled might bolt. She shrank back from them a bit as she held out the pouch, obviously expecting another caress and not wishing it.

"Here you are, my little mistress," Bruno said with utmost gallantry. He dropped his coin into the pouch and made a bow, careful not to touch her.

Her face lit up into a radiant smile, but Ursula frowned. Now that the child was close, she could see an enormous bruise purpling one cheek, and the thin arm that held her pouch was scarred by an angry red welt. The child must have had a bad fall. Ursula's fingers itched to soothe that swelling with a cooling poultice, but just at that moment their leader barked an order. The child's smile disappeared instantly, and she ran back to the woman to hide again behind her skirts. The minstrels bowed their thanks and melted into the shadows.

The next day, as they were riding out of the camp, Ursula looked back. The fields where they had stayed were flattened; crops were overrun and destroyed. As far as she could see, the ruined ground looked as if a plague of locusts had passed through. Not a blade or a leaf of anything green remained to be seen—everything had been either taken or trampled into the mud. Litter, refuse, and filth were strewn everywhere.

Not a very kind way to repay the villagers' generosity, she thought.

# Chapter 8

The minstrels joined the Crusade and sang every evening. The men drank and joked with any who would treat them to ale or wine, but the woman kept herself and her child apart. Ursula grew worried about the small girl. It seemed that no sooner did one bruise fade but another appeared. One evening the woman herself had a swollen lip, and her eyes looked as if she had been weeping. Try as she might, though, Ursula could find no way to speak to her. During the day the woman walked with the men, and after each performance at night she and her daughter seemed to just disappear.

April turned into May, and the farther south they went, the warmer it became. One afternoon, after they had made camp, Ursula determined to bathe herself as best as she could in the slow-flowing river. She had made do with pails of lukewarm water heated on their inadequate campfires long enough. The river's water would still be freezing, but at least she could wash her hair. She walked to the riverbank. Several women were already there ahead of her, however, washing pots and fetching water. She turned back downstream to seek out a more private place. As she pushed through a tangle of bushes on the bank, she heard soft singing. There, sitting on a patch of grass, was the young woman from the minstrels' group. Her daughter was in her arms. She was cradling the child, rocking her gently as she sang. Ursula stood for a moment, watching; then the woman saw her. She made as if to jump up.

"No, stay, please," Ursula cried. "Please don't go. I've been wanting to speak to you—I've enjoyed your singing so much."

The woman looked back at her, then beyond her as if to see if anyone else was there.

"I'm alone," Ursula said quickly, divining her thoughts. "There's no one else here. My name is Ursula," she went on. "We've come from Cologne."

The young woman hesitated for a moment before answering, and then timidly pointed to herself. "Elizabeth," she said. "My name is Elizabeth." She spoke the Germanic dialect poorly and with obvious effort. She looked down at the child in her lap with pride. "My daughter, Verity." The names sounded foreign and strange to Ursula.

"Where do you come from?" Ursula asked.

Elizabeth pointed north. "From far away. Across the sea. From England."

"Why are you here?" Ursula persisted. "Why are you so far away from your home?"

Elizabeth shrugged. "I follow my man," she said simply.

"That man—the one who is your leader—is he your husband?" Ursula asked.

Elizabeth's face clouded over. "No," she answered slowly. "My husband is dead. He died of plague. Lemmet is just my man. He takes care of me and my daughter. Without him we would have starved," she added. There was an odd note of defiance in her words. "He found us after my husband died. He took us in and taught me to sing. He takes care of us," she repeated.

As she was speaking, Ursula noticed an ugly, mottled mark on her neck.

Elizabeth saw her looking at it and hastily pulled the cowl of her shift up around it. "Lemmet has been good to us," she said, defiant again, as if Ursula had challenged her.

Ursula bit back the words she had been going to say. Instead, she turned to the child. "Verity," she asked softly. "Will you speak to me?"

"She has no German," Elizabeth answered quickly.

Ursula knelt, nevertheless. She reached out one hand slowly toward the child, as if luring a bird into her fingers. "Verity?" she repeated softly.

The child looked back at her, then up at her mother. There was another red welt on her shoulder. It had bled and was closing over in a pus-filled, dirty scab.

"I could heal that," Ursula said to Elizabeth. "I have herbs and poultices. I know how. I could ease the pain she must be feeling."

Elizabeth leaped to her feet and clutched Verity to her. "There is nothing wrong with her," she said. "It's just a scrape. Children get them all the time. You obviously know nothing!" She clasped her daughter's hand and glared at Ursula, then turned and almost ran out of the clearing, hanging tightly on to Verity.

Ursula, stung by the rebuff, made no attempt to call after her. She bathed and returned to their campsite, but she could not put the child out of her mind. The suspicion that Verity, and Elizabeth as well, were being maltreated by the man called Lemmet was strong.

Bruno noticed her preoccupation. Later that night, as they sat by the fire, he spoke to her.

"What worries you, Ursula?" he asked. "You've hardly said a word all evening."

Master William had gone as usual to the count, in spite of Ursula's protests. The count called for him nearly every evening now, with one complaint or another. Ursula suspected that there was not much really wrong with him, but having contracted for the services of a doctor, he was bound to use him. The strain was beginning to tell on Master William, however.

"My father," she answered. "I fear for his health. He gets so little sleep, and going back and forth to the count's campsite on these damp evenings is not good for him." She stopped speaking for a moment, then went on. "I was thinking, too, about that woman— you know? The singer with the minstrels? She and her child were down by the river when I went there."

"What passed between you to preoccupy you so?"

"The child always bears bruises—have you not noticed? And this afternoon the mother—Elizabeth she is called—had marks on her neck. I think that man who is their leader beats them."

"I have noticed," Bruno answered. "Did you ask?"

"No. I didn't dare." Absentmindedly, Ursula picked up a twig and threw it on the fire. "She is afraid. She would barely speak to me." She pushed the twig farther into the almost-dead fire with her toe. "I know not what to do about it."

"I do not see that you can do anything," Bruno said. "It is none of your concern."

"You, Bruno?" Ursula burst out. "You say such a thing? I would have expected better of you."

"You can treat the wounds if she will let you," Bruno said, "but I do not see what else you can possibly do. The woman chooses her own life."

"But she shouldn't allow such things to happen," Ursula argued hotly. "If not for her own sake, then for the sake of the child. She should leave him."

"And do what?" Bruno asked.

"I don't know. But she should do something! How can you not agree with me?"

"I do agree with you," Bruno countered, trying to keep a reasonable tone of voice, "but it might not be that simple for her."

"Simple or not," Ursula insisted stubbornly, "she should not stand for it. She should take better care of her child. I can't believe you to be so uncaring!" She jumped to her feet and once again retreated to her tent without bidding Bruno good night.

The mist was still hanging in the valleys when they set out the following day. The sun was out above it, however, and blazed a path across the water toward Ursula. She closed her eyes and raised her face to the warmth. It felt good, but her mind was still troubled and she felt even more guilty than before about Bruno. But he should agree with me, she thought stubbornly.

The next day it rained, and the day after that. For the rest of the time it took them to reach the Danube, the sun did not shine again. It got to the point where Ursula began to feel that she would never be dry or warm again. Everything they owned was wet. At night they crawled into a soaking tent and curled up in damp blankets. In the morning they drew on damp cloaks and climbed wearily onto the sodden seat of the wagon. Even Samson's spirits seemed diminished. They sought shelter in their tents as early as possible every evening, often with only cold bread and cheese to eat. The wood and branches they could gather were too wet to burn for a fire, and the incessant rain made it impossible for them to bother trying anyway.

The minstrels no longer sang, and Ursula had not seen them during the daytime. She was not even certain they were still with them. Her father's health was beginning to worry her seriously, however, so she tried to put Elizabeth and Verity out of her mind. She made infusions of mallow flowers and leaves for her father—the best remedy she knew for the unceasing cough that racked him day and night—and poultices of black mustard seeds for his chest, but nothing seemed to help. One night, just before they reached the Danube, the count sent as usual for her father, but when he tried to rise, he tottered. If Bruno had not been near to catch his arm, he would have fallen.

"You cannot go, father," Ursula said. "You are far too ill. The count will just have to do without you tonight."

"Daughter, I must," her father answered, looking around vaguely for his sack of herbs and medicines. "The count must have his nightly tisane. He cannot sleep without it."

"You *cannot* go, father," Ursula repeated. "The night air is foul with bad humors and dampness, and it will surely rain again before you can return. You must not go."

The old man looked at Ursula helplessly. "But the count will insist. What am I to do?"

"I will go. Tell me how to do it, and I will prepare his medicine and take it to him." Ursula reached into the tent and took up the bag.

"You? I don't know— The count will not be pleased—" Master William's voice faltered.

"It matters not one whit whether the count is pleased or not," Ursula replied firmly. "If he must have his medicine, then he will have to take it from me."

Determined as she had seemed, however, she did not feel so assured when she finally made for the count's tent. She had not seen the count since the evening before they had left, except at a distance. The memory of his austere, formidable presence hung in her mind. It was with a great effort of will that she called out to the man guarding the tent flap when she arrived.

"Who goes there?" the man answered suspiciously. "What do you want here, wench?"

Ursula flushed with anger. "I am Master William's daughter," she flashed back. "He is too ill to come to the count tonight. I have come in his stead to give the count his sleeping draft."

The man peered at her, raising his torch high so that he could see her face. At that moment it began to rain again.

"Wait here," he commanded. Sticking his torch into the soft earth beside the tent, he disappeared inside. It seemed like an interminably long time before he came out again. Ursula waited, getting wetter and wetter. To one side of the tent, a shelter had been erected and a fire burned underneath it. Several men crowded around it but made no room for her to shelter there as well. By the time the guard reappeared, Ursula was furious.

"You may come in," he said grudgingly.

Ursula swept past him into the tent.

This tent was enormous. There was room enough inside for six men to stand and move around with ease. The count was alone, however. He lay relaxed on a pile of cushions at the back. Dry cushions, Ursula noted. Her chin rose and her eyes blazed as she stared at him.

"Where is your father, girl?" the count asked. His tone was insolent.

"He is ill, my lord. He cannot come tonight." Ursula matched him insulting tone for tone.

"And am I, therefore, to be treated by a witch?"

"I am not a witch. My lord knows that as well as I."

"You are saying the archbishop lied?" The count's voice was now dangerously soft.

"I am saying the archbishop was given false information." Ursula held his gaze, willing herself not to drop her eyes.

The count turned away contemptuously. "I will not be treated by you. Go, and send Master William to me."

"He cannot come, my lord." For the first time her voice wavered. "He is ill. Truly, my lord, he cannot come out tonight."

He looked back at her. "You have my potion?" he asked.

"I have the herbs that he gives you with me. You can examine them yourself. All that needs to be done is to steep them in boiling water."

The count held out one hand imperiously. Ursula reached into the sack and pulled out a packet of ground-up leaves. She gave it to him, furious with herself because she could not stop her hand from shaking. The count opened the packet and shook a small quantity of the powder into his hand. He narrowed his eyes, peered at it suspiciously, and then sniffed it.

"It would seem to be my usual medicine," he said finally.

"It is, my lord. My father prepared it himself."

The count hesitated, then seemed to come to a decision. Ursula could see the desire in his eyes. The herbs were a mild sedative, but Ursula knew that at the count's insistence her father added a minute amount of ground field-poppy heads and their sap. Once a man drank of that, his need for it became greater and greater. Her father would not give it to his patients, usually, but the count had become accustomed to receiving it from his own doctor and demanded it. Ursula had only found out about it when helping her father prepare the mixture that evening—now she knew why the count insisted on her father's nightly visits.

When they finally reached the banks of the Danube, Ursula couldn't believe her eyes. All her life she had heard tales about this almost legendary river. She had imagined it to be immense and powerful, dwarfing even the Rhine, but in front of her now was a mere trickle of water: a stream barely two men's lengths wide and shallow enough to wade across with ease.

As they followed it eastward, however, toward the country of the Hungarians, the Danube began to grow. Other streams added their volume to it, the water deepened, and the channel widened until it became the impressive river that she had always believed it to be. It was wide and slow-flowing, however, with fields on either side instead of hills. This made the going easier for them and provided them with good campgrounds at night.

Another problem arose, however. The mood of the villages they made their way through was gradually changing. Tales had gone ahead of them, warning the townspeople of the great numbers who were coming their way and of the destruction and waste they left behind. Moreover, the Crusaders were now running low on food and supplies and were no longer content merely to accept what was offered to them. In a few villages there had already been ugly incidents of theft and the use of force by members of the Crusade to get what they wanted.

One night, when Ursula returned from Count Emil's tent, she found Bruno sitting up, waiting for her. There had been a strained tension between them ever since Ursula's outburst over Elizabeth and Verity, but Bruno seemed to have forgotten it at this moment.

"There is evil news," he said. They had been able to make a fire that evening in spite of a light rainfall during the day, and his face looked grim in the flickering shadows.

Ursula sank down beside him and stretched out her hands toward the warmth. She was exhausted and cold and hardly heard him.

"Do you remember that a nobleman named Walter Sans-Avoir, Walter the Penniless, started out from Cologne from his own party a full two weeks before us?" Bruno asked.

"Yes, I do," Ursula answered still too full of her own thoughts to pay much attention to his words. Her father did not seem to be recovering, and Ursula had had to minister to the count every night. The coldness between her and the count had not abated, but she was gradually losing her fear of him. In its place was a growing contempt. The man's weakness for her drugs demeaned him in her eyes. The long hours of driving in the wagon each day and the time she had to spend ministering to his needs, however, were taking their toll.

"It seems that Walter's men are suffering greater need than we are," Bruno went on. "When they reached Semlin, in Hungary, some of his men robbed a bazaar. They were captured."

Ursula looked at Bruno, suddenly alert. "Were they killed?"

"No, they were spared, but they were punished. They were stripped of their arms and even of their clothing. The men of Semlin hung the clothing on the walls as a warning, and to complete their humiliation, they sent the Crusaders naked across the river to rejoin Walter and his other soldiers. The townspeople of Semlin thought it a great joke, it seems, but Walter was enraged; he and his men are said now to be pillaging and ransacking the countryside mercilessly in revenge. Not even good Christians are safe from their fury."

"The townspeople will not welcome us when we arrive," Ursula said thoughtfully.

And, indeed, as they progressed they found the villagers increasingly hostile to them. Not only were they no longer offering gifts of food or supplies, but doors were actually closed against them. Supplies dwindled alarmingly. Within the camp, robberies were occurring nightly. Matters became so desperate that, without telling Master William, Ursula and Bruno began taking turns staying awake during the night to guard their few possessions. Samson barked and raised an alarm whenever strangers appeared, but after Ursula discovered a piece of meat thrown on the ground by their fire, she began keeping him inside the tent at night. Meat was far too precious to be thrown away. A dog who protected his masters might well be deemed enough of a nuisance to poison.

There was worse to come. Walter and his men raided and murdered without pity when they reached Belgrade. The commander of that city fought back, however, and the townspeople, maddened with anger and despair, trapped several of Walter's men in a church and burned them alive.

"In a church?" Bruno protested unbelievingly when they heard the news. His face was white, and he looked sick.

Ursula's mind leaped back to the burning of Jews in their temple in Mainz. Christians burning the Jews, now Christians burning Christians—Crusaders!

Was this what their holy pilgrimage was coming to?

"It seems you were right, Bruno," she said bitterly. "And this is still the beginning. I would not blame you if you did leave us now. You are not bound to stay." She honestly meant the words well, but they came out flat and cold. Bruno took them ill.

"You think I am so weak that I would leave you and your father as soon as danger threatens?" he burst out. "You must think badly of me for certain, then. I am sorry you have such a poor opinion of me."

"No! I meant not that! Please, Bruno—"

But this time it was Bruno's turn to stalk angrily away.

Late one night, soon afterward, Ursula sat alone beside the remnants of the fire. It was her turn to keep watch. The rains had finally stopped, and even the nights were warmer now; but in spite of that, she shivered and drew her cloak close. Everything seemed to be going wrong, and the future stretched bleakly before her. Bruno had withdrawn further and further into himself and would hardly speak to her. Every day, it seemed, there was word of fresh atrocities, and their own band of Crusaders was no exception. There had even been murder done within their own camp two nights before. And with every tale, Bruno's face hardened and changed until she felt she could barely recognize the carefree boy who had helped her carry Samson home so long ago in Cologne.

Suddenly, a rustle in the bushes startled her. She

leaped to her feet, ready to run, but a voice hissed out of the darkness.

"Please! Don't be afraid. It is only I—Elizabeth."

Heavily cloaked and hooded, a form emerged from the underbrush. Spilling out of the hood were long tendrils of golden hair. Ursula had heard the minstrels again in the evenings lately, but she had been too occupied with the count's needs to go and see them. Now Elizabeth stood in the shadows before her. In her arms she held the body of the child, Verity, limp and, to all appearances, lifeless.

# Chapter 9

**W**hat has happened?" Ursula reached for the child.

Elizabeth hesitated for a moment and then accepted Ursula's help. Together they carefully laid Verity down on the ground, and Ursula felt for the pulse of life that should be throbbing in the child's neck. For an instant she couldn't find it, and her heart sank. Then her probing fingers felt a flutter. It was weak but steady.

"Ursula! What's wrong?" Bruno had been awakened by the commotion and was standing over them.

Ursula immediately signaled him to silence. Elizabeth had started at the sight of him and looked as if she was ready to flee.

"It's all right," Ursula reassured her. To Bruno she said quietly, "Bring me father's herb bag out of the wagon. The child is hurt."

As she worked over her, Verity's eyes opened. She looked up at Ursula, and they widened with fright.

Elizabeth whispered to her quickly in a language Ursula couldn't understand. Verity clasped her mother's hand tightly, watching Ursula fearfully, but she lay still.

"I'll have to make a poultice," Ursula said. "Bruno, will you put a kettle of water on the fire to boil?" She turned to Elizabeth. "She has a bad bruise on one side of her head. How did it happen?"

"She fell." Elizabeth's voice was defensive. She kept her eyes on her child and would not look at Ursula.

Ursula decided not to argue the matter at the moment. She busied herself making the poultice and applying it to the child's head. When she finished, she looked over at Elizabeth.

"Stay here with me tonight. I must keep watch over her to make certain she does not sleep too deeply. It's dangerous after a blow to the head such as she has suffered."

"I cannot!" Elizabeth looked desperate. "Lemmet sleeps now—he doesn't know I'm here. I must be back by the time he awakens."

"Go, then, but leave Verity here with me."

"But—" Elizabeth began again.

"She must not be moved any more than necessary," Ursula said. "And she certainly must not be taken back within reach of that man." For a moment the two young women almost glared at each other. Then Elizabeth's eyes dropped again.

"What shall I say?" she asked weakly.

Ursula's patience gave out. "Tell him she's ill," she

snapped. "Tell him anything you want, but leave that child here with me."

Elizabeth looked as if she would argue further, but Ursula stared her down. Ursula might be the younger of the two, but it was clear she was the stronger. Elizabeth gave in. She bent toward her daughter and murmured a few soft words. The child immediately began to cry and clung to her. Elizabeth spoke to her again, gently disengaging her hands. When she rose, Verity made as if to go after her, but Ursula held her back. Just then Samson, alerted by the noise outside the tent, came out to investigate. He ambled over to the child on the ground, sniffed curiously, and licked her cheek. The child stopped in mid-cry and looked at him in astonishment. Then she looked up at Ursula. In spite of herself, the wonderment in Verity's eyes made Ursula smile.

"He's just a dog, child," she said gently. "Give him a pat. That's what he wants." She took Verity's hand in her own and passed it over the dog's scruffy head.

Verity flinched, but then, hesitantly, began to pat the dog on her own. Samson wagged his tail delightedly. Very slowly, a smile began at the corners of the child's mouth as well.

Elizabeth watched, then melted silently into the shadows.

The next morning Ursula was awakened from a light doze by the touch of sunlight on her face and the sound of birds singing. She had made a bed for herself and Verity the night before in the wagon, so as not to disturb her father. She looked quickly down at the child beside her. Although Verity had been restless for most of the night, she seemed to be sleeping peacefully now. Ursula had sung to her and talked to her, and Verity, at first fearful, had gradually succumbed. She slept now with one thumb in her mouth and the other hand wrapped tightly around a fold of Ursula's cloak. Bruno was already up and gone off somewhere, Ursula noticed. Probably to see to their horse.

"What is the meaning of this?"

A voice, guttural and harsh, jolted Ursula into complete awareness. She sat up abruptly, waking Verity as she did so. The child took one look at the man standing beside the wagon, let out a cry, and then burrowed closer to Ursula.

"Give me that child!"

Behind Lemmet, Ursula could see Elizabeth standing, twisting her hands together helplessly. Ursula was filled with fury.

"I'll do no such thing," she answered. "The child has been hurt. She'll stay with me."

Lemmet took a menacing step toward them. At that moment Bruno reappeared. He stepped between the man and the wagon.

"I think you'd best let them be," he said quietly.

"And who are you to tell me what to do?" Lemmet answered. His voice rose to a shout, and he raised his fists threateningly.

Bruno stood his ground, hands at his sides. "The

child has been badly hurt. The girl who tends her is a healer; she tends Count Emil himself. Perhaps we should take this matter to him?"

Lemmet, in the act of moving toward Bruno, stopped. Count Emil had an evil reputation among the Crusaders. He had had one of his own servants flogged almost to the point of death for spilling a horn of ale on him.

"The child belongs to me," he blustered.

"She does not!" Ursula broke in hotly.

"The child is ill," Bruno said quickly. "She cannot walk. If you take her from us, you will have to carry her. If you leave her here, we can care for her and let her ride in our wagon. When she is recovered, we can speak again about what should be done with her."

"When she is recovered, she will return to me!"

"When she is recovered, she—" Ursula began.

Bruno silenced her with a warning look.

Behind Lemmet, Elizabeth still hovered nervously. Ursula sent her a withering glance. Then she turned her attention back to Lemmet.

"I need that girl," he said. "She performs a useful service to me. Folk give more freely to a child."

"She won't perform if she dies," Ursula countered.

"She's not hurt that badly."

"She is. And if you take her from me, that will surely happen." Ursula saw Elizabeth gasp and turn pale. She looked away from her scornfully. Ursula was exaggerating, of course, but she felt no need to let Elizabeth know that. She had let this monster get his hands on her daughter—let her suffer the consequences of it.

Lemmet made up his mind. "Keep her, then. But just until she is well enough to get back to work. I don't tolerate useless people around me." He whirled on Elizabeth. "What are you doing here?" he roared. "Get back and see to our breakfast!"

With a last despairing look at her daughter, Elizabeth left.

Ursula turned to Bruno. "Thank you—" she began.

"You were very hard on that poor woman," Bruno said, cutting her off. "Have you no feeling for how she suffers?"

Ursula stiffened. "I feel for how her child suffers— and it is her fault!" She clutched Verity to her as Bruno began to gather wood for their morning fire.

How can this be, Ursula thought, watching him. We were such good friends in Cologne, but now—now it would seem that all we can do is argue.

Ursula kept Verity close to her and made her stay in the wagon, even after she was well enough to walk. She was afraid that if Lemmet saw her up and around he would come for her. The child still wept for her mother, but she was beginning to trust Ursula and doted on Samson, who returned the affection.

The next time Ursula saw Elizabeth was one evening a few days later when the minstrels were singing again around their campfire. Elizabeth caught sight of Ursula standing in the half-darkness, listening to them. Her voice broke in mid-song; then she recovered herself. She glanced quickly at Lemmet to see if he had noticed. Ursula backed into the shadows, not wanting him to see her. When the minstrels had finished and Elizabeth was collecting coins in her sack, she made her way cautiously over to the bushes where Ursula stood.

"My daughter," she asked breathlessly, looking over her shoulder to make certain that Lemmet was not observing her. "How does she?"

"She is well," Ursula replied. She would have turned away, but the remembrance of Bruno's words stayed her. "Really, she is well," she said more kindly. "We are taking good care of her."

"Thank you. Oh, thank you," Elizabeth said. "I can never repay you for your help. But when she is well enough, she must come back. You must bring her back to me. Lemmet insists."

Ursula stared at her unbelievingly. "You would take her back to be beaten again?" she asked. She could see a new bruise on Elizabeth's arm.

"If we're careful—if we do as he says and don't make him angry—" Elizabeth stuttered. "He's a good man—really. He just can't help himself if we make him angry—"

Ursula made a sound of utter disgust and turned her back on the woman.

"What would you have me do?" she heard Elizabeth wail behind her. "Who else would take care of us? Who else would provide for us?"

\* \* \*

They reached Hungary hard on the heels of Walter Sans-Avoir's men. The city walls came in sight and on them, displayed for all to see, were the weapons and what was left of the clothing of the sixteen men who had robbed the bazaar. The gates of the city were firmly closed against them. No one came out to greet them.

That night, as Ursula entered Count Emil's tent, she was surprised to hear voices. Usually at this time he was alone. She was even more astounded to realize that the other man there was Peter the Hermit. The holy man of Amiens was standing at the back of the tent, facing the count. His eyes were blazing.

"They must supply us!" he shouted as she hesitated in the doorway. "They must give us whatever we need! We are God's holy army. We are on the most holy of all pilgrimages—on the pope's own Crusade!" In the more than two months that had passed since he had first entered Cologne, he had learned enough of their dialect to speak it without an interpreter, but his words were so wild and incoherent that it was almost impossible to understand him.

Ursula backed out hastily. She waited until she saw him leave before she approached the tent again. When she entered this time, the count had thrown himself down on the velvet-covered straw pallet that served as his bed.

"Give me my medicine and leave," he snarled at her savagely.

Ursula complied and left as quickly as possible. At

their campsite she found Bruno sitting with his back against the wagon where Verity slept. Forgetting the uneasiness that had been between them lately, Ursula hurried to tell him what she had overheard.

"I'm afraid, Bruno," she finished. "The Hermit looked insane with fury, and the count—I have never seen him in so foul a mood. Something terrible is going to happen—I'm certain of it."

"There are mutterings in the camp as well," Bruno answered. "People are hungry and angered that the townsfolk will not aid them."

Ursula climbed into the wagon, curled up beside Verity, and clasped the child to her tightly. Her heart pounded in her chest. From the tent, she could hear her father coughing incessantly. Bruno stirred restlessly by the fire.

The next morning on her way to the riverbank to wash out their breakfast pot, Ursula pushed through some bushes, only to stumble upon two men. One was a soldier, the red cross crudely stitched onto the shoulder of his uniform. The other was obviously a villager. The villager was holding a pair of old leather shoes—worn and ripped out at the toe.

"That's robbery!" the soldier cried.

"Take it or leave it," the villager answered. "You'll not do any better. Not around here. We don't want the likes of you rabble here, and the sooner you clear out the better!"

"But you promised me new shoes. For the price I paid I should have good sound shoes—these are trash! I want back the payment I gave you!"

The villager laughed and threw the shoes into the dust at the soldier's feet. "Then you'll have to come and get it," he said mockingly. He turned on his heel and headed back for the village.

Within moments a crowd gathered around the soldier. Resentful mutterings soon gave way to curses, and those in turn gave way to shouts. Before Ursula could realize what was happening, the number of soldiers had swelled alarmingly and more were pouring in. Soon it seemed as if the whole camp was on the move.

"Justice!" she heard one cry.

"Revenge!" cried another.

"We'll teach them to cheat soldiers of God!"

Then, before her horrified eyes, what seemed like the whole army of soldiers that accompanied them took to their horses and galloped in a furious storm toward the city. She ran back to their campsite.

"Bruno!" she gasped, as she saw him watering the horse. "The soldiers have gone and they're storming the city!"

Bruno reacted at once. "If that's so, there'll be fighting. Quickly, we must strike the tent and pack. If the fighting reaches here, we must be ready to move at once."

Verity began to cry. Ursula scooped her up and lifted her onto the wagon into her nest of rugs. She collared Samson and dumped him in beside her.

"Don't cry," she said, using every effort of will she possessed to make her voice calm. The child couldn't understand the words, but she could understand a frightened tone of voice only too well. Ursula patted her for a moment, then made signs to her that she was to hold Samson. The tears stopped. Thumb in mouth, Verity clutched the dog and huddled into the blankets. Ursula looked at Bruno.

"Elizabeth?" she asked. "Where could she be? Should we look for her?"

"There might not be time. We must not get separated. God willing, she will come to us before anything starts. If not—" His words trailed off.

Master William had heard and was already out of the tent and starting to carry things to the wagon.

"Master," Bruno said, "please sit and rest. Ursula and I can do all that's necessary."

But the old man seemed not to hear him. He stopped and gave Bruno a confused look. "Fighting?" he asked. "There ought not to be fighting." Then he doubled over with a paroxysm of coughing. Ursula looked despairingly at Bruno as she reached for her father's arm.

"Father," she said gently, "please do as Bruno says. We'll load the wagon, but you must save your strength."

Her father looked back at her. "What is happening, child?" His voice wavered. "This is not the way it was supposed to be."

At noon they were still waiting. Elizabeth had not appeared. Others in the camp had also taken fright and were hastening to pack up their belongings. No one seemed to know what was going on. Once, Ursula saw Count Emil come out of his tent and confer briefly with the Hermit. They turned worried glances toward the city and then went back into Peter's tent and did not come out again. The majority of the soldiers had been in the mob that stormed the city, and many of the ordinary men, inflamed by the riot, had run after them, brandishing cudgels and any other weapons they could get their hands on. As a result, the camp had a strangely deserted, expectant air.

It was early afternoon when a shout was finally raised from the road leading to Semlin. Almost immediately, the thunder of horses' hooves was heard, and a cloud of dust billowed into the air. The soldiers charged back into sight. Many were bloody and bore the marks of a furious battle. Some swayed in their saddles alarmingly, but every one of them was cheering. They rode into the center of the camp and began throwing sacks onto the ground.

"Grain!" they shouted. "And turnips! Meat! Clothing! Supplies for all!"

"No one can stand before us—now they know what happens to those who will not give to us freely!"

Peter the Hermit came out of his tent, closely followed by Count Emil. The Hermit held up his hands in an effort to bring quiet and order. The gesture was useless. With a roar, the people surged forward. Sacks were ripped open, grain spilled on the ground. Men and women fought and clawed to get as much of the foodstuffs and clothing for themselves as they possibly could. Cloaks were torn, bread trampled into the dust. Fights broke out all over. A man grabbed a sack of something—he probably had no idea what—and began to run with it toward Ursula and Bruno. Another tripped him up and grabbed for the bag. As Ursula watched, paralyzed with shock, the first drew out a dagger and plunged it up to the hilt in the second man's back. A soldier, still hot and inflamed with battle lust, rode by and saw him do it. Drawing his already bloodstained sword, he lunged and cut the assailant down. Then he rode off, howling his battle cry.

Ursula stared at the sack on the ground in front of them. Blood from both men was slowly seeping into it. She turned away and vomited. Bruno was at her side in an instant. He held her while she tried to pull herself together. From somewhere he produced a scrap of cloth and gave it to her. She wiped her mouth with it and spat out the last bitter taste of bile.

"There will be retaliation," he said to her then. "We must get back to the wagon."

The camp was now in utter confusion. The Hermit and the rest of the noblemen were still vainly trying to call for order, but it wasn't until the last of the booty had either been snatched up or trampled into uselessness that the general insanity subsided. Then the word was passed quickly: "Four thousand Hungarians have been killed! They are massing for revenge. Move out! Move out!"

This time Ursula and Bruno were among the first

of the wagons to leave. The nobles and the soldiers had formed up hurriedly, and the long train began to move, even as men were still straggling back along the road from the city. Many of them carried sacks and stolen clothing, but no one now thought to fight for it. The enormity of what had occurred was just beginning to be understood.

Four thousand killed.

Ursula's mind was blank with horror.

# Chapter 10

t was not so much a march as a headlong flight. They didn't even dare stop to make camp that night, but forged on until they reached the Sava River where it crossed the Danube and put it between them and the Hungarians. Only then did they feel safe. When they reached Belgrade, they found the town deserted. The people of the city had heard of the massacre in Semlin and had fled to the mountains. Peter's army took advantage of this to pillage the city.

"When the townsfolk come back, they will find nothing," Bruno reported bitterly to Ursula. "The city has been sacked completely."

"Bringing more ill will upon us," Ursula answered. "Our crimes are mounting, Bruno. When will we have to pay for them?"

"Soon, most likely," he answered.

The successful eluding of the Hungarians and the sack of Belgrade combined to raise the spirits of the soldiers of the Crusade enormously. Confident now that the Hungarians would not be able to catch up to them, and assured that the Bulgarians were too fearful to deny them anything, they set out along the road to Nish triumphantly. They had to leave the Danube here, however, as it turned sharply eastward, and the road to Constantinople lay more to the south. For the first time since leaving Cologne, they no longer had a river to carve a path for them. The way now lay through heavy forests with only the occasional clearing and village. At night wolves howled again, and the underbrush was alive with the sounds of animals hunting. Bears roamed these forests, and wild boar. One night, as they huddled around their fire, Ursula heard the scream of an animal somewhere in the blackness beyond their small circle of light. She shuddered and drew Verity close to her. Only that day, they had found a woman in hysterics in one of the tiny villages they had passed through. Wolves had taken her child, they said.

They reached Nish in seven days. By that time everyone was exhausted. The food they had stolen from Belgrade was gone, and hunger once again became a daily way of life. It was a vast relief, then, to hear that, in spite of what they had done, the Crusaders were to be allowed to camp outside the city for a few days, and the governor, Nicetas, would provide food for them. As security that there would be no repetition of the sacking and pillaging, however, he had taken two hostages: Geoffrey Burel and the Frankish Walter of Breteuil.

To Ursula's surprise, no sooner had they made camp than the townspeople began to swarm in, bringing food and even alms to many of the poorer pilgrims. For the space of this short time, it seemed that sanity had returned to the world. With the food and rest, even Master William's health began to rally. Ursula's hopes rose as she saw him doing more and more of the daily tasks and becoming more cheerful. He even began to talk confidently again about their mission.

"We are over halfway to Constantinople, daughter," he said. "Soon we will be there and I will see it. The most wondrous city in the world, it is said. And then—then, on to Jerusalem. Is it not marvelous, Ursula? God's will is surely with us. I am certain that the worst is over now."

In all the time since they had fled from Semlin, they still had not seen Elizabeth. Ursula and Bruno began to fear she had been lost or killed. That night, however, she finally came, distraught, to their campsite.

"My daughter," she cried as soon as she saw them. "How is she? Lemmet would not let me leave before—I think he thought I meant to flee in all the confusion. I was so worried about her. Where is she? May I see her?"

"She is sleeping," Ursula answered. "Let her be for now. She is well. I promise you," she added quickly, putting out a restraining hand as Elizabeth made a move for the tent.

"Thank God for his mercy," Elizabeth said. "But

Lemmet wants her back. Now that calmer times seem to be upon us, he wants to continue our concerts, and he wants Verity to collect coins. He will not be denied."

Ursula was incredulous. A wave of hot, possessive anger swept over her. She could feel again Verity's frail body pressed against her, see the terror in her eyes. "I nursed her and made her well. We protected her. I will not let her go back to that man!"

"He will come and take her. He will kill you if you do not let her return." Elizabeth looked at Ursula desperately. "I mean what I say. He—" She stopped for a moment. "He has killed before," she went on in a low voice. "I have seen it."

"I can believe it," Ursula spat out. "And he will probably kill Verity if she returns."

"No! I'll be more careful. I'll take better care of her." Elizabeth's whole body was shaking. "She's my daughter!" she cried. "I'll take care of her—I promise!"

"As you've taken care of her so far?"

Just then Verity heard her mother's voice. With a cry, she was out of the tent and into Elizabeth's arms. Elizabeth clutched the child tightly to her and bent her head over her daughter's. Her tears fell on the pale hair, her eyes implored Ursula.

"I will not let her go back," Ursula said. Her voice was adamant.

In the end, Elizabeth was forced to give up and leave without taking the child. Watching her go, her shoulders bowed and shaking, Ursula was seized with pity. Then she tightened her lips and her face hardened. Lemmet was not going to beat Verity again, even if it cost Ursula her own life. She saw Bruno standing in the shadows, watching.

"You think I am cruel to that poor woman," she said defensively. "What, then, would you have me do?"

"I know not," he answered.

Geoffrey Burel and Walter of Breteuil were released; the company made ready to start on their trip again. As they took their place in the train, however, Ursula and Bruno were overrun by a large group of angry men. They pushed past on the narrow trail, stumbling against the wagon.

"Too good for their boots," Ursula heard one of them grumble.

"Think they're better than honest pilgrims, that they do," another agreed.

They staggered as they strode by; their words were loud and slurred. Ursula realized they were drunk. They were filthy, their beards unkempt, and their clothes looked as if they had not been seen to for weeks. The red crosses that had been clumsily sewn on their shoulders hung in tatters. Their voices rose as the grumbling turned to shouts—they were fueling each other with their anger, leading each other on. Several of them were carrying torches. At this point the road crossed the ford of a river. In the clearing around the ford sat a small mill.

"That's the place!" one of the men suddenly shouted. "That's the miller there who thought he was too fine for the likes of us!"

"Too fine for us, is he?" yelled another. "We'll show him!"

At once, a chorus of shouts and insults rose into the air. With one accord the group of men turned away from the river and ran toward the mill, torches flaming. They threw two torches onto the thatched roof of the building, the others at and around the wooden sides.

Bruno had just led their horse into the river moments before the outcry began. He looked back, startled, but the current, weak though it was, took all his attention.

"What's happening?" he called out to Ursula.

She twisted on the wagon seat to look, trying to make sense of what was going on.

"They've torched the mill!" she cried. "Those men! They've set fire to the mill!"

The building blazed up immediately. A woman carrying a baby ran out of it, two small children after her. A man followed. The man ran desperately to the river with a bucket, dipped it in, and ran back to throw water onto the flames. The effort was useless. Ursula watched helplessly from midstream while the men responsible fled and splashed noisily across. Not one other Crusader still on that side of the river made a move to aid the miller and his family.

Peter the Hermit and the leaders were already far up the road on the other side, well out of sight. There was no way they could know of what had happened; there was nothing Ursula and Bruno could do except maintain their place in the line of wagons. By the time they reached the other side of the river, the mill was enveloped in flames, beyond any hope of being saved. Ursula took up the reins, but she let the horse follow the others automatically. She, Bruno, and Master William watched the plume of black smoke rising until they were out of sight.

"Nicetas is a stern commander," Bruno said finally. "He was more than patient with us, I think. More than forgiving. I fear that he will not let this go unpunished."

Nicetas did not wait long. Before noon of that day, a company of men rode furiously past them toward the head of the train. Rumors flew back thick and fast. Nicetas had attacked the rearguard before they could ford the river. There had been fighting. He had taken hostages but was not satisfied with that—he was coming after the main body of Crusaders.

Ursula realized that the pace had quickened. She had to urge the reluctant horse almost to a trot to keep up. Then, suddenly, a cloud of dust arose from way in front of them. Hooves thundered. A whole section of Peter's soldiers and guards, howling war cries, galloped back toward them, past them, and on to the rear to do battle with Nicetas.

After that, all was thrown into confusion. The

people panicked. Wagoneers urged their horses into a gallop and thundered past Ursula and Bruno, their wagons sometimes perilously close to colliding. The people on foot at the rear dropped their bundles of food and supplies as they ran to keep up.

Ursula whipped the horse on, but he was an old horse, not capable of more than what he was doing. Verity, behind her in the wagon, began to cry. Master William took her in his arms. It was a measure of her terror that she let him hold her—she had never let anyone but Ursula near her before. Samson cowered beside them.

"Bruno, what are we going to do?" Ursula whipped at the horse again, caught up in the panic.

"Hope the rearguard can hold off Nicetas's forces," Bruno answered grimly. "Make that horse go as fast as you can, Ursula!" He grabbed up a cudgel that he kept by the front seat of the wagon and turned to watch the road.

Behind them, as far as he could see, was a flood of terrified humanity. Ursula looked back quickly over her shoulder and saw a wagon suddenly lurch off the path and overturn. It was immediately submerged by the wave of fleeing people. She urged the horse on again. By now the beast was going at as close to a gallop as he could. Their wagon was bouncing and jolting in the ruts so hard she feared they would turn over as well, but she dared not slacken the pace.

Suddenly screams broke out, just out of sight

behind them. Then a band of Nicetas's soldiers appeared. They rode through the running people, swords slashing mercilessly. People fell and were trampled by other people fleeing over them.

"Bruno!" All of Ursula's concentration was required to keep the horse under control, but she couldn't help another quick glance back. At that instant the soldiers reached the first of the wagons and Ursula, horrified, saw a soldier lean from his horse and slice his sword deep into the chest of the man who was driving it. The man collapsed and his horse, panicked by the noise and the smell of blood, bolted. Before Ursula could look away, it overran the wagon ahead and charged into the horse that pulled it. Both horses went down; both wagons disintegrated in a confusion of splintering wood and screams.

The soldiers were checked by the wreckage, but only momentarily. They swung out around it and began to cut a new swath through the people on either side.

"Pull off!" Bruno shouted.

Ursula looked at him in astonishment.

"Pull off!" he shouted again. "We can't outrun them—we've got to get away!" He pointed at the thick trees to the right of them. "Pull the wagon over as close as you can to the trees; then we'll make a run for it!" He turned to Master William in the back. "Give me Verity as soon as we stop, master," he yelled. "You'll have to jump off and run for the trees. Do you understand?"

The old man nodded. In all the confusion, he seemed almost calm. "Give this to Ursula," he called back and passed up his bag of herbs and medicines to Bruno. "We will need it."

Ursula wrenched the reins to the right. The horse, too panic-stricken now to know what was happening, followed the command blindly. They jarred over the stubble that bordered the road. Ursula had a moment of fear that they wouldn't be able to stop before they reached the trees. A vision of the wagon crashing into the thick forest rose sickeningly in her mind. Then, at the last possible second, she threw every ounce of strength she had into pulling back on the reins.

*"Whoa!"* she screamed. For one disastrous moment she thought they were lost. But the horse swerved and finally halted, his sides heaving and soaked with sweat.

Bruno tossed over her father's bag and in the same motion reached back for Verity. Ursula leaped off the wagon and reached up to help her father. The old man jumped down with surprising agility, Samson close behind. They tore for the trees.

They ran without stopping for breath, as far into the forest as they could, but they couldn't outrun the screaming. It went on and on. Ursula dropped to her knees and covered her ears with her hands, but she couldn't shut out the sound.

Finally it stopped. And then there was a deathly silence. Bruno, Master William, and Ursula stared at one another. Verity clung to Ursula.

"We must stay here until all danger is past," Bruno said. They were well away from the road, but even so he whispered. Ursula nodded.

As night fell they huddled together, sheltering one another as best they could with their cloaks. They didn't speak. Only Verity slept.

They didn't stir from their hiding place until dawn broke the next morning and the birds began to call sleepily in the trees around them. Ursula winced as she stood up. She was cold—the damp seemed to have seeped right through her and into her bones. She ached in every joint and muscle. As she looked anxiously toward her father, he, too, roused himself and began to cough. The coughing shook his frail frame so much that he could not speak.

"We must get back to where we left the horse and wagon," she said to Bruno.

He didn't answer.

"It might still be there," she insisted. "It's possible that they've left it." Bruno's face told her how unlikely he thought this to be.

They wakened Verity and started back through the trees. Samson trotted at their heels. Even he seemed subdued. Aside from the birds now singing lustily in the forest around them, there was only that same ominous silence. As they drew near the edge of the forest and began to tread more cautiously, they stopped speaking and listened intently, but there was nothing to be heard. None of the usual noise of the awakening of a camp of thousands that had filled the air every morning since they left Cologne, no sounds of priests saying masses. They emerged from the woods and looked around cautiously. At first there was nothing to be seen. Then Ursula gasped. Their wagon was almost where they had left it, but it lay on its side, the wheels smashed beyond repair. Ursula ran toward it, forgetting all caution, but came to an abrupt halt with a cry of despair. The horse lay on the ground in front of the wagon, still in his traces, dead.

"Why kill him?" she burst out. "Why would they kill a horse?"

"They couldn't take him, I suppose, and they didn't want us to have him," Bruno answered. His voice was bitter. He rummaged through the ruination in and around the fallen wagon. "They've spoiled all our supplies. Didn't even take them—just made them unfit for us. I don't know if we'll be able to salvage anything."

Ursula turned away from the dead animal and went back to help Bruno. She couldn't talk. There were no words to express what she felt.

Together, with Verity hindering more than helping, they searched through the mess for something that would still be edible. Their sack of grain had been slit open and was spilled over the ground. Ursula found a small pouch and gathered up as much as she could. At first she tried to avoid picking up dirt as well; soon she gave up and just dumped everything in together. Sticks, lumps of earth—she'd separate them later.

Master William rummaged around in what was left of their clothing.

"They've slashed everything," he said. The note of confusion was back in his voice; his face was blank and hopeless again. After his brief burst of energy the day before, his body now sagged with weariness. He gave up his search and slumped to the ground, his back against the ruin of the wagon. "There's nothing left." He shook his head slowly from side to side. "Nothing left! And we were so close, so close I thought I would see Constantinople—and Jerusalem. Am I never to pray in our holiest of cities now?"

Ursula wanted with all her heart to reassure him, to vow that his dreams would come true, but how could she? This, surely, was the end. She and Bruno rescued what they could and piled it in a heap. It was pitifully small.

"Dare we make a fire?" she asked Bruno. Then another fear hit her. "The flints! The tinder!"

"It's all right," Bruno answered. "I made certain to take them with me when we fled."

They collected twigs, wood—even bits of the demolished wagon—and soon had a small blaze going. It didn't offer much warmth, but just the sight of it was comforting. Ursula sat her father down beside it and then retrieved a piece of blanket and wrapped it around his shoulders. He hardly seemed to notice what she was doing.

"We must find water," she said.

"First we had better see what has happened," Bruno said grimly. "See where all the others are."

The road itself from which they had escaped the day before lay hidden behind the slight rise they had bumped over so desperately. Ursula looked toward it.

"I'll go with you," she said, but she was filled with dread. The silence— What would they find? "Do you think it's safe now?"

"I think so," Bruno answered. "There would be no reason for Nicetas's men to stay around. They've had their revenge."

Leaving Verity with Master William, and Samson tied to the wagon with a bit of cord that Bruno had salvaged, they climbed over the rise. Ursula took one look at what lay before them and her heart seemed to stop. As far as she could see, bodies littered the road. Men, women, children—all scattered as if carelessly flung by some giant hand. Wagons were overturned and demolished. The bodies of horses, donkeys, and cows lay among the bodies of the people. Blood was everywhere. And now Ursula became aware of the smell. A smell like the stench of the butchers' alley in Cologne.

"It's not possible!" She couldn't look away. "Isn't there anyone left alive at all?" Her voice rose, close to hysteria. Beside her, Bruno stood frozen.

As if in answer to Ursula, there was movement on the other side of the road. The ground sloped steeply up into the mountains there. A small knot of people was emerging timidly from the shelter of the trees. They, too, stopped when they saw the carnage in front of them. Then they looked across at Bruno and Ursula, but in silence. No shouts or greetings were exchanged; no one spoke.

# Chapter 11

radually, more and more figures came forth.
Some searched among the bodies; others
just wandered aimlessly, stunned. Priests
made their way from body to body, giving
what blessings, what absolutions, they could. There
was a large clearing on the side where Bruno and
Ursula stood. The people began to collect there. For
the most part they had nothing but the clothing on
their backs, but some of them carried bundles and
hastily wrapped parcels. Many of them were wounded
and bleeding.

A figure emerged from the trees farther down the
road. It was a man riding a donkey, and Ursula recognized Peter the Hermit. No arrogant guard surrounded him now, although a few men followed him.
Next, a group of horsemen emerged from around a
bend in the road. Count Emil was in the lead. He
slumped in the saddle, and his normally proud face
was pale and haggard. He caught sight of Ursula and
Bruno and rode up to them.

"Ah," he said to Ursula, "so you survived, did you? That is well for me. Do you still have your medicines?"

Ursula nodded. She could not trust her voice.

"We will make camp here for this day," he went on, a trace of the old authority returning. "I doubt Nicetas's soldiers will return. There is no more sport for them here now. Later, when we are settled, you will come to me. I need your care." There was a long gash on one cheek, and blood seeped from the shoulder of his tunic. Ursula nodded again. The count moved away from her, toward the Hermit.

Ursula turned back to Bruno. He reached out a hand to her. Together, they returned over the rise to the wreck of their wagon.

The fire had gone out, though Master William, sitting beside the ashes, seemed not to realize it. He didn't answer when Ursula called out to him.

"He must have food and something hot to drink," Ursula said to Bruno. "So must the child. Can you light the fire for us again?"

Bruno just nodded. He still seemed incapable of speech.

Her father did not ask what they had found; Ursula did not tell him.

This time they made a larger fire. Together, Bruno and Ursula unhitched the body of the horse and dragged it as far as possible into the woods. Ursula saved two battered pots from the wagon. "What shall we do for water?" she asked. She was suddenly aware of a raging thirst.

"There's a stream a ways back. I noticed it before," Bruno said finally. His voice was wooden. "Give me one of those pots and I'll fetch some." He took the pot and disappeared with it. When he returned, Ursula gave some to Verity and her father and then drank deeply herself. The cold sweetness of it was a shock. Then she set the pot on the fire to boil. She began to clean the grain as best she could. There were no vegetables left and no meat. They would have to make do with gruel. She measured the kernels out carefully, trying to gauge how long the amount left would last. There was no telling when they would be able to get more.

After she had fed her father and Verity and made up a soothing tea for Master William, she allowed herself to start thinking about what they were going to do. They couldn't stay here—they couldn't go back. They would have to go forward, but without the wagon they would have to walk. Her father was too weak for that, she knew. Perhaps some of the wagons had been saved. Perhaps she could arrange with Count Emil to see that her father was allowed to ride. The count owed him that, surely. She picked up her medicine bag.

"I must go to Count Emil," she said. "I'll see if he will help us."

Bruno just nodded. Like Ursula, he had not eaten.

Ursula had to brace herself to go back over the rise between them and the road. She hurried toward the place where Count Emil and the Hermit had set up their camp, trying as much as possible not to see the bodies strewn along the way. It was impossible, however, and at some points she even had to pick her way among them. By the time she reached Count Emil's fire, her chest was burning with the effort of holding in her grief. Campfires had sprung up at the edges of the woods and people huddled around them, binding their wounds and eating what food they had managed to salvage, but everywhere there was still that same eerie silence.

The count glared at her as she stepped into the circle of his fire. "What took you so long, witch?" he snarled, obviously in pain. Ursula didn't react to the epithet. It was meaningless now. Without being asked, she prepared an infusion of the count's medicine for him to drink first, even though it was only midday. He snatched it and gulped the liquid down thirstily, not seeming to notice or care about the heat of it. She had found some butterbur in a stream they had crossed only a few days earlier and had collected the leaves and roots. It was just as well, she thought, as the supply of herbs was dwindling rapidly. Butterbur was especially good for skin wounds. She applied a poultice to the wound in the count's shoulder, then showed him how to apply more of the cure to the gash on his face. The count submitted to her ministrations impatiently.

Ursula held her tongue as long as she worked, but when she had finished and the count was resting more comfortably, she could keep silent no longer.

"My lord," she began tentatively.

"Yes?" He glanced at her sharply. "Are you not done now?" he asked.

"Yes, my lord," she answered. "But there is something—something I would ask of you."

"What?" he barked.

"My father, my lord. He is very ill, as you know, and our wagon has been destroyed. If we are to go on, he cannot walk. Is there a wagon in which he might ride?"

The count snorted. "If we are to go on? Of course we are to go on! We are not to be conquered this easily. But there are no wagons for your father to ride in. None. They are all destroyed, most of the horses killed or stolen. What horses there are left will be for the soldiers and those of us who lead you, witch, as is altogether fitting. Your father will walk. Like all the rest of you rabble, your father will walk. And if he continues to be too ill to come to me, then you will continue to do so. I have paid for his services; I intend to receive them, one way or another."

"But everything you gave us, my lord—everything is gone!"

"That is hardly my fault. I've lost my own wagon as well. The Hermit has lost his—" His face darkened.

Ursula had been about to remind the count of the silver coins he still owed her father, but she was abruptly silenced. If it were true that the count had lost his own wagon, this would not be the time to beg for the money. And if Peter the Hermit had lost his wagon—Ursula remembered the rumors of the chest of money that he carried in it to buy supplies for the Crusade. If that was gone, too—

"Begone, witch. We will march tomorrow for

Constantinople, and I expect you to report to me after the evening meal as usual."

Ursula started back to Bruno and her father without another word. Once she would have flared back in anger at the count's words. Once she would have burned with fury to be spoken to so. She stepped carefully around the body of a young man. Once— How long ago had that been, she wondered dully. Surely it had been years ago. Surely it had been a lifetime ago.

They left at dawn the next morning. With the rise of the sun came the warning of just how terrible the stench of the aftermath of this battle would be in a few hours. There was no possible way to bury so many, although here and there some were trying to do so.

They had just started out, Bruno carrying Verity and Ursula supporting her father, when they came upon a woman sitting, keening by the roadside. The body of a man lay beside her.

"They've killed him," she moaned. "They've killed my husband and taken my children." She rocked back and forth in her agony.

Ursula stopped beside her. She leaned down and rested a hand on the woman's shoulder. "Come with us," she said softly. "We have a little food left. Come with us. We will help you."

"How can I leave? I cannot leave!"

Try as she might, Ursula could not convince her.

Finally she took off her cloak and wrapped it around the woman. "God be with you," she whispered. "The true God—not the God of these wolves we travel with."

And wolves the Crusaders seemed as they marched down the road through Sofia to Constantinople. Of the more than twenty thousand who had left Cologne, fewer than seven thousand remained, and, like a pack of hungry animals closing in on any prey they could find, they attacked everything and everyone that came within reach. It was every person for himself or herself—no one shared their plunder. Those who would not plunder, such as Ursula and Bruno, went without. In the evenings when she tended to the count, he would sometimes give Ursula a handful of grain or a few spoiled vegetables, and that was what they subsisted on. When she begged for more, telling him that her father was dying, his face turned cold and closed.

"He has been well paid. It's not my fault that he lost it. I can afford no more."

She didn't even bother to ask for the silver owing to them—there was nowhere to spend it now. Villagers ran at the sight of them.

The way grew even more wild and mountainous, with dark forests closing in on all sides of them. Walking became more and more difficult; the ground was never level. They were either climbing upward or descending rocky, narrow trails that at times seemed to barely cling to the sheer mountainsides. They forded icy mountain streams and picked their way around washouts on the steep paths where one false step or slip would send them hurtling to their death far below. At night they slept huddled in their cloaks and in the remnants of the blankets they had saved. They tried to keep the fire going all night to keep at bay the beasts they could hear hunting in the dark. They had used up the last of their grain, but they had to stay on guard to keep those even more desperate than they from stealing the few things that remained to them. Verity cried for her mother, but Ursula, although she had asked around and looked for Elizabeth constantly, had not been able to find any trace of her. The other minstrels, including Lemmet, seemed to have vanished as well. Master William grew weaker each day.

One night, when Ursula had just returned from tending to the count and had checked her father, who was sleeping in exhaustion by the fire, a noise in the bushes startled her. Bruno was not there. Samson barked and dashed to her side as she caught up a heavy branch. Verity, who had been trailing after her, took shelter behind her skirts.

"Who's there?" Ursula demanded. Desperation had given her courage, and she felt little fear. Anyone who came to rob them would pay for it dearly.

A figure stumbled, almost falling, into the circle of firelight. Ursula could see the ruins of a blue woolen cloak hanging in tatters around the woman's shoulders. Verity suddenly let out a cry and, before Ursula could stop her, tore across to the woman. At the same time Ursula recognized Elizabeth. Her hair was hanging in filthy strands, and her face was mottled with dried blood and dirt. She seemed unable to talk, but she reached out her arms to Verity and enfolded the child within them.

Bruno came back, carrying water. Since the massacre he had not spoken more than necessary, and Ursula had been too frightened by the grimness of his face to try and find out what he was thinking or how he was feeling. Now, however, the tight, deeply etched lines around his mouth and eyes lightened somewhat. He put the water down hastily and hurried to support the woman.

"Elizabeth," he cried. "We feared you dead!"

"Come," Ursula added quickly. "Sit down by the fire. Let me help you."

She gave her the last bit of thin soup they had been saving for breakfast and then gently began to bathe her face. Elizabeth was bruised and beaten; there was a long gash on her forehead.

"Lemmet—" Ursula began scathingly.

"No," Elizabeth answered. Her voice was weak, and it obviously cost her an effort to speak. "It was not he. Not this time. As soon as rumors began that the soldiers were about to attack us, he and the others disappeared. They just left. I know not where they have gone, nor even if they are still alive."

"How came you by all this, then?" Ursula asked, but of course she knew the answer.

Elizabeth stroked Verity's head as the child nestled

in her lap. "A soldier," she said simply. "He caught me as I ran. He beat me and wounded me when I would not submit to him willingly, but then he got drunk and I escaped as he lay sleeping. I have been searching for you ever since. I was so afraid for you—for Verity—" She stopped, her voice breaking. "Then I found a poor woman sitting by the roadside. She told me she had seen a girl of your description traveling with a boy, an old man, a dog—and a child! She told me you had given her your cloak. She said you were an angel."

"First witch, now angel," Ursula muttered. "Each about as unlikely as the other. The world has surely gone mad."

"I followed after as quickly as I could, and then today, after everyone had made camp, I found someone who could tell me where you were." She bent her head down to her child. "It's a miracle that I've found you. A miracle that we're all still alive."

The next day they camped beside a turnip patch. It was well tended and obviously belonged to someone, but there was no one around. Ursula looked at it. Her father and Verity both desperately needed nourishment. With Elizabeth's return, they had another person to feed. Her own stomach was cramping with hunger, and they had nothing left at all in their camp. She hesitated no more than a minute and then walked into the field. It wasn't until she had begun digging up the turnips and filling the pocket she had made of her skirt that she realized Elizabeth had followed her.

"You are still weak," Ursula said shortly. "I can manage this."

"I want to help," Elizabeth answered simply. "There is little enough I can do to repay you for that which you have done for my daughter and me."

"There's no need—" Ursula began, but she was stopped by the look in Elizabeth's eyes.

"I want to help," Elizabeth repeated. "And if it's possible—now—I would be friends." She smiled.

Ursula felt the iron noose of pain that had been constricting her chest loosen. She straightened up. The burden of turnips suddenly seemed lighter. She looked back at Elizabeth.

"Yes," she said finally. "Yes, I would like that." She put out her hand and Elizabeth took it.

They collected enough turnips for their pot that night and as many as they could carry with them on the road. As they emerged, laden down with the stolen vegetables, Ursula saw Bruno looking at her. There was an odd expression on his face. Suddenly, she remembered the young boy they had seen in the marketplace about to lose his hand.

"If he valued his hand so much, why did he steal?" she had asked, certain that the punishment was just, certain that stealing was unforgivable.

Did he have a child to feed? A father to keep alive? Had his stomach been hurting as much as hers? She dropped her eyes from Bruno's and flushed.

Two nights later she knew that her father could go on no longer. Bruno had almost had to carry him that day, and when Ursula had tried to get him to sip a little of the weak soup and hot tea she had made for him, the liquid just dribbled back out of his mouth. By the time she settled him down, wrapped in Bruno's cloak as well as his own against the night dew, he was delirious with fever and did not recognize her. He sank into a restless, confused slumber. Ursula sat over him, watching.

"Go to the count, Bruno," she said finally. "Tell him that we will not be able to travel tomorrow. My father cannot go farther and I will not leave him."

Bruno left. Verity and Elizabeth slept, wrapped tightly in each other's arms. Ursula tried again to get her father to sip the tea, but again with no success. She settled back to watch over him. Suddenly, without warning, he sat bolt upright and called her name.

"Ursula!"

She was at his side immediately.

"Lie down, father. Do not try to speak."

"No! I must tell you—" He forced the words out, then gave in to a fit of coughing that seemed to last interminably.

"Hush, father. You must rest." Ursula tried to soothe him, but he only became more agitated.

"The wolf—the wolf—" Her father's eyes stared; he made an enormous effort to speak further.

"What wolf? There's no wolf, father." Ursula held him tightly. The shaking shoulders felt more fragile than Verity's.

"Calm yourself, father. Do not disturb yourself so."

"You must—" The old man would not give up the struggle. His eyes fixed on Ursula with the frantic need to speak. "You must look to the wolf. . . . The wolf, daughter . . ."

His eyes closed and he sank back into Ursula's arms. He began to mutter incoherently. She lowered him to the ground and rearranged the cloaks snugly around him, but he was deep in delirium again.

"The count will give us no help."

Bruno came quietly back into the firelight and looked down at Master William. "He says that if your father is too ill to continue he must be left at the next village and you must go on."

"I will not," Ursula answered. "I will not leave my father."

But, as it turned out, she was forced to. The next morning when she knelt beside him and touched his shoulder to waken him, he was dead. Sometime during the night, while she had dozed fitfully beside him, he had simply stopped the struggle to breathe. For him, now, the journey was over.

Not, however, for Ursula. The count sent them two men so that she and Bruno could bury her father, and a priest came to give him absolution. They laid him in the shelter of an ancient elder tree. The elder tree was a magic tree, so many healers believed. The mother under whose protection all herbs grew and thrived. It was a special tree, full of the love of mankind.

"Protect my father's body," Ursula prayed. "Speed his soul to God." There was an aching, tearing pain in her chest. Her mind was full of memories. Of her father. Of her mother. Of her brothers. All of them gone now. Hot tears spilled down her cheeks. She felt Bruno's hand seek out her own, and she grasped it tightly. "Grant him peace," she added as the dirt gradually covered the shallow grave and the priest murmured his blessing. There would be no peace for her, she knew.

They packed up their meager belongings. In a very few days, so the count's men told her, they would be in Constantinople.

Ursula said farewell to her father as she trudged out of sight of his grave and then turned her face forward again. But in her mind she was looking back—back along the trail they had left behind them, all the way to Cologne. The trail of ruin, destruction, and death.

# Chapter 12

I t was a pitiful remnant of the Crusade that finally reached Constantinople in the heat of summer, more than three months since they had left Cologne. Ursula would never, for the rest of her life, forget her first sight of the famed and fabulous city. They walked down from the hills, and the plain upon which the city sat came into view with the sparkling, impossibly blue waters of the Bosphorus shining beyond it. Above the massive city walls, domes and steeples almost too numerous to count were etched against the sky. Beside her, Bruno drew in his breath. The walls stretched endlessly ahead of them. Never had she imagined a city of this vastness.

Emperor Alexius of Constantinople—emperor of all the Byzantine Empire—was in sympathy with the Crusaders, despite their maraudings. He would dearly love to receive Jerusalem back into his realm. He was wary, though, and insisted that the Crusaders camp in sparsely grassed fields on the slopes outside the city walls. Only manageable, strictly controlled groups of a few people at a time would be allowed inside. Obedient to his orders, the townspeople welcomed them warmly, and supplies were brought out to them. Soldiers were set to guard them, however, and the sun beat down mercilessly. The few trees around gave little or no shade; even the nights were hot beyond endurance. The people suffered with the heat and grew restless and irritable. The news that Alexius had given Peter money toward the rest of the journey failed to appease them. Talk began to grow that they should be given more—that they should be given free access to the city. Soon, discontented members of the Crusade began to sneak in and steal whatever they could lay their hands on. They broke into palaces and villas and took the very lead from the roofs of the churches. The soldiers guarding them became hostile; the shopkeepers and townspeople began to fear them. Not surprisingly, Alexius decided that it was time for them to move on.

"Now I must get my silver from the count," Ursula announced when they heard the news. "This will be our last chance to buy supplies before we leave. The emperor has been generous—the count should be able to afford it now."

Bruno, however, was dubious. "He has never said he would give it to you, Ursula. You should not count on it."

"I will get it from him," Ursula repeated stubbornly.

She returned less than an hour later, her face a mask of fury. Elizabeth stared at her in alarm.

"What has happened?" asked Bruno.

Ursula glared at him. She had bitten through her bottom lip and a trickle of blood flowed down her chin.

"He refused! He lied! He swears that he already gave my father the silver. In fact, he accuses me of lying to try and get more!"

"He would give you nothing?"

"He gave me a few copper coins. I threw them back in his face!"

"Oh, no!" Elizabeth gasped.

"Even copper coins would purchase us what we need," Bruno remonstrated.

"Do you think I would accept them from him? I told him that I would have the full amount or I would not treat him again."

"And what did he say to that?" Bruno's voice was unnaturally quiet.

"He laughed! He laughed at me and said, 'We'll see about *that*, my witch.' Then he had his guards practically throw me out of his camp."

"You were foolish—" Bruno began.

Ursula took a step forward and hit him across the face as hard as she could. In the stunned silence that followed, she turned and fled into the nearby trees.

It wasn't until much later that night, long after the rest of the camp had gone to sleep, that Ursula crept back to their campsite. Elizabeth and Verity were curled up together in a blanket to one side. The fire was banked low but still burned. Bruno sat beside it. Ursula approached him. He looked up.

"How can I apologize?" she whispered. "The only reason you are here is because of me. You have done so much for us. What can I do?"

Bruno reached up a hand to her and pulled her down beside him. He held her close. "There's no need," he said quietly.

For the first time on the whole journey, Ursula began to cry. She wept, and it seemed that she would never be able to stop.

The next evening two of the count's men appeared at their campsite before they had even finished their evening meal. In spite of herself, Ursula felt a jolt of fear.

"You are to come with us," one of them said.

Unprotesting, she rose and they led her away. Again, within an hour she was back.

Bruno leaped to his feet when he saw her. Ursula spoke, forestalling any questions. "He still lies," she said dully. "He will not pay me what he owes in honor."

"What did he do?" Bruno asked.

"He gave me back the copper coins I had thrown at him, told me I must continue to serve him, and that he was being more than generous and fair with me."

"What did you do?"

"I accepted them."

\* \* \*

They were shuttled across the shining expanse of the Bosphorus as quickly as possible and resettled at Civetot, on the shore of a wide plain that jutted out into the Sea of Marmora, a prudent distance away from Constantinople. There the emperor ordered them to wait until the main body of Crusaders, who had left Cologne at the appointed time, caught up with them. They were explicitly ordered not to penetrate any farther into Asia until the reinforcements arrived, but as the weeks dragged by, the Crusaders grew restless and impatient.

One morning the camp was awakened by the commotion of a large party of soldiers riding in. Ursula stepped out of their makeshift shelter to see. The soldiers were well armed and rode fresh horses. Chain mail and harness fittings gleamed in the sunlight. At their head rode a tall, dark-haired man astride a giant warhorse.

"That's Walter Sans-Avoir!" Bruno exclaimed. "I like this not."

A knot of foreboding formed itself in Ursula's stomach.

Her fears were well grounded. With the arrival of this Crusader, who had shown himself to be so greedy and vicious, the soldiers in Peter's party began to raid again. They began close to the camp, but with each success they ventured farther afield until, by summer's end, they were pillaging and fighting in the lands of the Turks themselves.

Then, early one morning, came news that they had

sacked villages in the very suburbs of Nicaea, the capital of the Turkish sultan himself. They had stolen herds and flocks and massacred all villagers who opposed them, Christian and Turkish alike. The Turks, enraged beyond all endurance, were marching on Civetot.

"They intend to murder us all!" the cry went out.

It was a group of Count Emil's own men who came for Bruno. "Every able-bodied man must fight," they shouted, as they pressed a sword into his hand. Bruno stared at it as if it were evil incarnate that he held. Ursula ran to his side.

"He cannot fight!" she cried. "He's a stonemason— a builder of churches—not a soldier!"

"He's a soldier today." Their leader laughed, and he prodded Bruno none too gently with his spear. "Follow us," he commanded. He herded Bruno away with his horse. Bruno turned for one quick, agonized look at Ursula and then was pushed out of sight.

Ursula stood, staring after them unbelievingly. All around the camp the same scene was taking place. Men shouted in anger, women shrieked, but all to no avail. Before the sun had fully risen, the whole army of Crusaders had marched out of the camp. All that were left behind were old men, women, children, the sick, and the priests.

"Ursula! What's going to happen?" Elizabeth, still rubbing sleep from her eyes, came up behind her. Verity clung to her skirts as she had done when Ursula had first seen them.

"I don't know." She reached automatically to comfort the child, but her eyes were fixed on the road down which Bruno had disappeared.

They didn't have long to wonder. A scant few hours after the Crusaders left, dust on the road in the distance drew everyone's attention. Almost immediately, they could hear shouts and screams. A horde of charging horses and men running on foot suddenly appeared, tearing back toward the camp as if their lives depended on it—as they did. Behind them now appeared a terrifying spectacle. The Turkish army was pursuing the Crusaders, swords drawn and flashing, arrows flying through the air. In the sunlight their cloaks and turbans shone in a rainbow of colors—the glint of silver and gold was dazzling.

Ursula only had time for one horrified look before the mob was upon them. With the sea at their backs, there was no place to run. Verity was by her. She scooped her up into her arms. Elizabeth jumped up from the fire where she had been sitting and ran to them. They shrank back against a tree and clutched each other.

The whole world seemed to explode into noise around Ursula. She held tightly to Elizabeth and Verity and buried her face in Verity's hair. The child was shrieking—a high-pitched, shrill, unceasing sound that cut through the screams and the deafening war cries around them. Ursula felt herself hit by the shoulder of a horse. She staggered and would have fallen had it not been for Elizabeth. She dared a look up and saw a swollen, raging face under a scarlet turban. The Turk's horse was charging straight at them, his scimitar flashing down toward them in a curving gleam of light. She shut her eyes and cringed, waiting for the blow.

Elizabeth made a queer, muffled noise and suddenly crumpled. Unprepared for it, Ursula lost her balance as well. She toppled heavily onto Verity; Elizabeth fell onto her. Verity's shrieks stopped as suddenly as if cut off. Ursula lay, face pressed into the ground, waiting for the final blow. Horses' hooves thundered by her ear; she could feel the vibration of their impact on the earth in front of her face. Another jolt shook her body, but, strangely, she felt no pain. Verity was quiet. Too quiet. Ursula didn't know if she had fainted or had been killed. She moved to take some of her weight off the child, but then froze back into stillness as she heard yet another horseman charging toward them. This time the horse leaped over their pile of bodies, one rear hoof sending dirt flying on top of them.

Gradually the screams and cries died down. Ursula still didn't dare move. There was silence and then the sound of horses' hooves again. Ursula opened her eyes and tried to see what was going on without moving her head. All she could see around her were bodies— bodies lying silent and still. A group of Turkish horsemen rode into her view. One rode directly toward her. As he approached, Ursula closed her eyes again. She didn't even dare breathe as she sensed the man on horseback looming over them. After what seemed like an impossible length of time, she heard him move off.

Still she lay frozen. It wasn't until the noises were long gone that she dared open her eyes again. As soon as she moved, Verity began to whimper. The child was crushed under her and must have been near suffocation. Carefully, Ursula pushed aside the weight on top of her and eased Verity out from underneath. She cast her eyes around continuously, on the alert for any signs of returning horsemen, but there was nothing. Suddenly the realization dawned on her that the weight she had pushed aside was Elizabeth. The woman was lying beside her now, sprawled in an ungainly position. Ursula knelt to feel for the pulse in her throat, but as she did so she realized it was useless. At the same time, Verity sat up and saw her mother. Then she looked at Ursula's face. She screamed, and screamed again. Ursula reached up a hand to her own cheek. It was covered with blood. Elizabeth's blood.

Ursula reached for Verity and held her tightly. The child struggled futilely and screamed without ceasing. Ursula clutched her even more strongly and hid Verity's face against her breast. She heard a weird, keening sound. It took several moments for her to realize that it was she herself who was making it.

# Chapter 13

rsula was brought back to reality by a cold nose thrusting itself into the palm of her hand. At first she wasn't even aware of it, but finally a low whining forced its way through to her consciousness.

"Samson!"

The dog cowered beside her. He was covered with dirt. There was no way of knowing how he had survived the battle, but indeed he had. He licked Verity's hand, but the child, who had stopped struggling and now lay limp in Ursula's arms, made no response.

Suddenly, Ursula became aware of a man standing a few feet away from them, staring at them. She clutched at Verity and cringed away from him, but he stood as if not really conscious of where he was, his face blank. With a feeling of disbelief, Ursula recognized Bruno.

"Thank God," she managed to get out. "You're alive!"

"Are you all right?" He spoke the words slowly, through stiff lips.

"Verity and I are. Elizabeth—" She choked.

Bruno knelt beside the body and, still as if in a daze, gently smoothed the matted hair back from Elizabeth's brow.

It was only then that Ursula looked around. The carnage on the road to Sofia was as nothing compared to the sight that now met her eyes. The field was covered with bodies. Nowhere else was there any sign of movement. The waves that lapped at the shore behind her ran red, and corpses floated aimlessly in them, bumping onto the stones of the beach, then drifting out again. She looked back up at Bruno helplessly.

"Is everyone dead?" she whispered.

"Nearly all," Bruno answered. "Peter the Hermit survived—he was in Constantinople with the emperor. A few of the other nobles and their men escaped and have taken refuge in a tower. They are hoping to be rescued."

"And the Turks?"

"They have withdrawn."

"Count Emil—what of him?" The questions were automatic. Ursula's mind was still blank with the horror of it all.

"Dead. I saw him fall."

"So this is the end of it?" Verity stirred in her arms, and Ursula clasped her ever more tightly.

"This is the end of it."

"What shall we do?"

"I have two horses. We can flee to the tower and take refuge there with the others, or we can take the horses and try to make our own way home."

"Where—where did you get horses?" Ursula was still deep in shock. It was hard to make sense of what Bruno was saying.

Bruno shrugged. "I stole them. From one who had no more need of them."

"Oh," Ursula answered dully. "Yes. Of course." Then Bruno's words seemed to sink in. "I don't want to go to the tower with the others, Bruno. I want no more to do with any part of this Crusade."

"I feel the same," Bruno said. He stood up and passed his hand over his brow, as if to wipe it clear. "We'll make our own way back, then."

They buried Elizabeth under the tree where they had been standing. Without tools, they had to scrape at the earth with their hands and could only manage the shallowest of graves, but they did the best they could and covered it with stones picked up from the beach.

"We should have a priest," Ursula said.

"There are none left alive," Bruno answered.

Ursula closed her eyes and bowed her head. "God bless her," she whispered. "God's grace be upon her and receive her into heaven." Such a short life. Such an unhappy one.

Alone, the three of them made much better time than had the full party. That was fortunate because winter came early in the mountains, and they had to cross them before the snow came. People were kind and took pity on them. They gave them food, shelter for the night, and even clothes for Verity. Ursula accepted everything offered with a mute thankfulness. Pride was no longer an emotion she could afford. As the days passed, however, she became more and more distraught. The child, Verity, would not speak. Ursula tried to talk to Bruno about it, but after the horror of the battle at Civetot, he had withdrawn into himself until it was almost as if he were a stranger to her. During the day he did what was necessary for them, but at nightfall he wrapped himself in his cloak and sat by the fire for hours, staring into the flames. Nothing Ursula said seemed to reach him; most of the time it seemed he did not even notice if he ate or slept. He bore no wounds on his body from the battle, but Ursula feared he bore wounds on his soul instead.

One evening they heard the wolves again. The weather was cold and clear, and the sound carried piercingly to them. Ursula reached down to tuck Verity's blanket more securely around her and then drew her own more closely around herself. She shuddered.

"Wolves!" she exclaimed. "I hate them!" She looked up at the dark masses of the woods behind them. Trunks and branches of trees were etched against the darkening sky like jagged scars of black lightning. The wolves called again.

"Wolves are much-maligned beasts, I think," Bruno said suddenly. "They are loyal to their own kind and only kill out of necessity to live. That is more than can be said of men."

Ursula was startled. It was the first he had spoken

for days, but the words were heavy with bitterness and cold with contempt. It sounded nothing like the Bruno of old. She drew a deep breath.

"During the battle, Bruno—" she said hesitantly, afraid of what she was going to ask. "Did you have to kill?"

"Yes," he answered. "In spite of all that I believed, in spite of God's holy will, I killed. When I was about to be killed—I killed first."

In the light of the fire, Ursula saw that his face was bleak.

"But you had to," she said. "You were forced to. Surely God will forgive you. You are not like the others!"

"Am I not?" Bruno asked. "I think I am. I think I have no right even to ask for forgiveness."

"No, Bruno—you must not think that. Look what you have done for us. Without you we would most certainly have perished. Pray! God will forgive you—I know he will."

"I cannot pray."

A short while after Yuletide they saw the walls of Cologne in the distance, church towers rising above them. The first snow was finally falling. The bells of Cologne were ringing. They were home.

But what was home? Ursula's heart sank when they rode down the street of the apothecaries and came in sight of her house. It was just as they had left it—a pile of burned-out rubble.

As they stood there staring, Mistress Ingrid bustled out of her house, her eyes starting from her head at the sight of them.

"It's like seeing someone back from the dead!" she exclaimed. "We'd heard you'd all been murdered by the heathen—truth to tell, I never expected to see you again! But I kept an eye on things for you, just as I promised your father I would. You'll find all as you left it. I even fed your cat for you." She smirked with satisfaction.

The cat chose that moment to slink out of the ruins. Samson let out a bark and rushed after it joyfully. Ursula looked at Mistress Ingrid warily.

"And Master William," the woman burbled on. "Where is he?"

"My father is dead," Ursula answered.

"Oh, dear! Such a shame! Such a wonderful man he was." She looked askance at Bruno and Verity, who held Ursula's hand, staring straight ahead of her, unseeing. The child had yet to speak a word or react in any way to Ursula's many entreaties.

"But it seems you've got yourself quite a family now, haven't you?" she poured on. "I recognize the boy—he was around here before you left, wasn't he? But where did you find that little one?"

"Her mother died as well," Ursula answered. "Verity stays with me now."

Bruno had been tethering the horses, ignoring Mistress Ingrid's torrent of words. He turned to Ursula. "I'll return in the morning," he said woodenly.

"I must see if my hut is still standing, but I will be back to help you tomorrow."

Before Ursula could say anything, he walked away. She looked after him, suddenly overwhelmed with a sense of loss and emptiness as he disappeared around the corner.

"And will you be opening the apothecary again?" Mistress Ingrid was still talking on.

"I don't know," Ursula answered shortly. She had lain awake many nights on their return journey, wondering how she was going to live. To open the apothecary again would take more money than her share of the horses' sale would give her.

"Well, it's a delight to see you back, that it is," Mistress Ingrid exclaimed. She positively beamed at Ursula.

Ursula was confused. Why was the woman being so friendly? The last time she had seen her, she was all for having Ursula burned as a witch.

"What—?" she began, stopped, then gathered her courage and continued. "What has happened with Mistress Elke?"

"Oh, her!" Mistress Ingrid grimaced with distaste. "She's dead, too. Died of the pestilence soon after you left. It's said now she brought her own curse upon herself with her evil tongue and sharp ways. In any case," she added quickly, "your sins are pardoned now. You have been on the Crusade!"

So that was it. Ursula stared past the woman toward what was left of her house, but she wasn't seeing that.

In her mind she was seeing a field full of bodies; a road strewn with dead children; the shallow, stone-covered grave of a friend; the deeper resting place of her father; the child, Verity, who could not speak; and Bruno, who could not pray.

Yes, she thought, I've been on the Crusade. And for that I am now cleansed and pardoned of my sins?

The sale of the horses brought enough money for wood to make a new roof for Ursula's house and to repair Bruno's hut, which had fallen in during his absence. A year before, someone would have taken possession of that hut before his return, but Cologne, these days, was strangely empty. So many had left for the Crusade, and the pestilence had been particularly bad during the last few months.

Bruno quickly found work with his old master on a new church they were building, but, to Ursula's despair, he remained sunk in depression. He helped clear the rubble from her house, built the roof for her, and installed new shutters, but nothing she could do or say comforted him. He had confessed to his priest. His priest had absolved him and even blessed him for taking part in the Crusade, but Bruno remained convinced of his guilt.

Ursula cast around for means to support herself and Verity. She began doing errands for her neighbors, cleaning other stores, washing—anything that would earn her a few coins. She spent as little as possible and gradually began to accumulate enough to start replenishing her herb supply at the market. She found the neighbors surprisingly kind and sympathetic. The very ones who had been first to shout "witch" before now regarded her almost as a saint. Even Britta and the other girls made cautious attempts to regain her friendship. Ursula was the first to return from the Crusade. The fact that it had failed and they had never reached Jerusalem seemed not to matter; all that was important was that she had gone.

While she was working in her neighbors' houses, her neighbors often asked her about the foreign lands she had seen. Was it true that all the domes and towers of the churches in Constantinople were sheathed in gold? Was it true that the people wore jewels of such weight and quantity that they couldn't walk and had to be carried everywhere on litters? Ursula answered as best she could. Telling what they wanted to know was a way of repaying them for their kindness and acceptance of her, but the remembering was like a continual reopening of a festering wound.

News reached them, finally, that the remaining Crusaders who had taken refuge in the tower had indeed been rescued. They were now back in Constantinople with Peter and had joined up with the forces for whom the emperor had bidden them wait in the first place. This Crusade was mightily armed and made up of great armies of nobles and their soldiers. They were making ready to set out for Jerusalem and this time were certain of success, the news said. Ursula would not even listen to the tidings.

Verity grew no better either. She sat wherever she was placed or occasionally crept into a corner and huddled there. She allowed herself to be fed and taken care of but stared with blank eyes and made absolutely no response. Ursula spent a part of each day teaching her German words, pointing out objects all around them and naming them, but there was no way of knowing whether the child heard or not.

Spring came, and, to Ursula's joy, the garden at the back of the house began to come to life. With Verity seated on a blanket beside her, Ursula threw herself into weeding and tending the overgrown herbs. And then, one day, Bruno burst into the house with a vigor and eagerness Ursula had not seen since they had left Cologne. She looked up, and her heart leaped to see his deep blue eyes shining.

"Ursula!" he cried. "I have been made a carver! No longer just a mason, hewing out blocks for the church—I have been chosen to work on the baptismal font itself! It is to be carved all around with scenes from the Bible, and *I* am to do it. The master says my work is a glory to God!"

Ursula dropped the shift she was mending and rushed to him. "Bruno—what wonderful news!"

He grabbed her by the shoulders and enveloped her in a hug. Then, suddenly, his face became serious again.

"Ursula, do you think—? Could it possibly be that . . . that this is the way I can work for my forgiveness from God? Through giving him the best work from my hands and heart that I can?"

Ursula lifted her hands to cradle his face. The hope in his eyes—the light in them again—was almost heartbreaking. She caught her breath with a sob.

"Oh, yes, Bruno. Of course it is. It must be." She passed her fingers gently over the deep creases in his brow. "Everything will be all right now. It will!" She drew his face down to hers. The kiss surprised them both. They looked at each other, startled, and then laughed at the same time at the wonderment each saw in the other's face.

# Chapter 14

hey were wed on one of the first soft days of summer. It was a simple marriage. They walked together to Great St. Martin's, Bruno carrying Verity. The priest heard their vows, and they walked back home again. For a wedding feast they dipped into their small supply of coins and added meat to the nightly stew.

The garden thrived, and soon Ursula was harvesting her herbs. Bruno rebuilt the shelves alongside the hearth, and she drew greater and greater satisfaction from watching them fill up with bags and sacks, and hanging swatches of drying leaves and flowers. Finally, one day, Bruno lowered the front shutters before he left for his work, and Ursula set out her wares. The apothecary was open again.

That night, as they sat by the fire, Samson suddenly sprang up with a bark. Horses' hooves clamored on the cobblestones outside. Ursula called sharply to stay him—he still hadn't learned any sense about horses—but he ran to the door in a paroxysm of whining and tail-wagging. A knock rang out, the door opened, and a figure walked in. Samson went mad.

"Ursula? Master William? Are you here?" The voice was deeper than Ursula remembered, but there was no mistaking it. David!

Ursula sprang up. David was a hand taller than when she had last seen him. He was dressed sumptuously, and a cloak of heavy scarlet wool hung from his shoulders. He looked so much more like a young man now, and so much less like the small boy she had known, that she stopped, suddenly shy. Samson, however, threw himself upon his master.

David knelt to tousle the dog's head. "Samson! I hardly dared hope he would still be alive." He looked up at Ursula and Bruno with a happy smile. "I'm here with my father," he said, "to reclaim my uncle's house from the archbishop. My father has already gone to see him, but I couldn't wait to come see you. Where is Master William? And what has happened to the house?"

"David! I can hardly believe it is you! But here, sit," Ursula cried, pulling a small coffer forward. "I have so much to tell you, and I want to hear so much from you. But first—" She sobered. "I must tell you— My father is dead. He died last summer. On the Crusade."

David's eyes clouded. "I wanted to see him again," he said. "To have him meet my father. To thank him for what he did for me. I am so sorry, Ursula." Then he seemed to hear what else Ursula had said. "On the Crusade?" he asked. "Went you on the Crusade with those *to'im?*"

*To'im*—"aimless wanderers." In such a way did the Jews speak of those who had persecuted them so heartlessly.

Ursula met Bruno's eyes. "We will tell you of that later," she answered. "It was a thing of necessity, not of choice. But I want to hear of you. How did you get back to Mainz? What happened to your family there? We heard that only a handful escaped."

"We were among that handful," David replied. His face darkened, and Ursula guessed that his memories were no less painful than her own.

She reached out a hand to him. "I feared for you. I am so thankful you were spared."

They talked long into the night. Samson remained glued to David's feet the whole time. For the moment, Ursula had forgotten about Verity. The child had crept into a corner near the open trapdoor to the cellar. Suddenly a piercing scream brought them all to their feet.

"Verity!" Ursula cried, but she was nowhere in sight.

"In the cellar," Bruno said. "The cry came from the cellar."

They rushed down and found her, unhurt but cowering in terror, staring at the wall above her. A grotesque animal's head, carved into the wall here, hung out over her. The light from the fire, coming in through the trapdoor, caused its shadow to flicker and move on the wall behind it.

"Wolf!" Verity screamed. "Wolf!"

Ursula ran to her and gathered her into her arms.

"It's just a stone wolf," she soothed. "Just a carved wolf . . ." Then two realizations struck her at the same time. The child had finally spoken—and she had shrieked out "wolf." Her father's last words came back to her. Unconsciously, she repeated them aloud.

"Look to the wolf." She stared at the carving. "Look to the wolf."

"What are you saying?" David broke in.

"My father—" she said slowly. "As he lay dying he said that. 'Look to the wolf.' I knew not what he meant."

David went over to the wall and reached up his hand to place it on the beast's muzzle. "He meant this wolf. It guards the door."

Ursula was confused. "What door? What do you mean?"

"Did he never tell you then?" David asked. At Ursula's shake of the head, he went on. "Do you remember when your father hid me? You couldn't imagine how we managed to conceal ourselves here in the cellar."

"Yes, I remember," Ursula answered, still bewildered.

"There is a door here," David went on. "A hidden door. And underneath this cellar there is another secret cellar. He never told you that?"

"No," Ursula answered. Her voice trembled. "Unless—unless that is what he was trying to tell me at the end. But how do you open it?"

"The wolf," David answered. "The wolf holds the key. Bruno—fetch a light for us and I'll show you."

Bruno was back in an instant with a lighted wick floating in a dish of tallow.

"Come here," David said.

Bruno brought the light to the wall, and they clustered around him, Verity clinging tightly to Ursula. The flame cast even more fantastic shadows—the other carved heads danced on the walls around them.

"Something or someone of great value must have been hidden here once," David said. "The opening of the door is marvelously contrived. Watch." He pressed his hands against the neck of the wolf. Ursula gasped as the head and the stone upon which it was carved suddenly began to swing outward. Inside the dark opening, they could just make out a ladder leading down into what seemed to be a black hole.

David took the light from Bruno and started down. "Come, follow me," he called back.

Ursula passed Verity over to Bruno and then clambered after David into the musty dankness of the secret cellar.

The walls here were rougher than those of the cellar above, rubble pressed together rather than cut stones. Ursula recognized the building method from the walls surrounding Cologne itself.

"Roman," she murmured. The cellar must have been dug in Roman times and then the foundations of their own house laid on top. Her eyes were drawn away from the walls, however, when the light revealed what was in the cramped room. A straw pallet lay in one corner, and a table and chair sat in the middle.

"My father always said this was the house where

Emperor Henry was hidden when he was a boy," she whispered. "I thought he imagined things, but maybe he was right." Then she caught her breath as she saw something else. On the table lay a deep green velvet pouch. She moved swiftly over to it. Her hand reached out, hovering. Hardly breathing at all now, she forced herself to pick it up—and forced her mind to stop the wild imaginings that had suddenly taken hold of her. The pouch jingled and sagged in her hand. As if—as if it was filled with—

Bruno called anxiously down to them. Ursula's head burst up through the opening.

"He did pay my father! He was telling the truth. God forgive me for disbelieving him. Count Emil was telling the truth!" She reached up her hand and a cascade of silver coins, gleaming in the wavering light, poured out onto the floor at Bruno's feet.

"Why did your father not tell you sooner?"

They were back upstairs, Ursula still holding the pouch unbelievingly. David stared at it.

"Why would he have left it there in the first place?" he asked.

"He must have felt there was too much danger of losing it if we took it with us," Ursula answered. "And he was right; we would have lost it." She paused and then went on. "He must have meant it to be here for us to start with anew when we returned. He wasn't himself those last few days before we left—so much had happened. I imagine this was all he could think of to do. But then he became so ill. He grew so confused. When he finally tried to tell me, he couldn't."

Verity snuggled up to her and raised her face questioningly. "Not a real wolf?" she asked timidly. "Down there—not real?" She stumbled over the German words.

Ursula hugged her tightly. "No, my pet. It's not real. It's a carving. Like what Bruno does. Only not so pretty," she added, laughing. Then her face became serious, and she stared down at the pouch in her hand.

"I sought this for so long," she said. "So desperately. And now that I finally have it—"

With a sudden gesture she held the pouch out to Bruno.

"Here. Take it. Tomorrow carry it with you and give it to the priest. Let it be given to God."

Bruno reached out to accept it, his eyes questioning.

Ursula looked around at the warm, firelit room, heavy with the scent of her herbs. She looked at David with Samson lying at his feet. She felt Verity's soft cheek nuzzling into her neck. Then she looked back at Bruno.

"I already have everything I need," she said.

**Karleen Bradford** was living in Germany when she discovered that the People's Crusade left from Cologne. Intrigued by the event and its potential for a story, she began to research the Crusade in detail. Eventually she and her husband decided to drive the route the Crusaders took, traveling through countries such as Hungary and Bulgaria, and ending in Turkey.

Karleen Bradford has written many award-winning books for young readers. A Toronto native, she has lived in England, Germany, the Philippines, Colombia, Puerto Rico, and the United States. She now lives in Ottawa, Canada.